After reading A Lil' Somethin' on the Side, you are now ready for...

A Lil' Somethin' More

Printed in the United States of America

First Edition

BISAC Fiction / Motivational & Inspirational

10 9 8 7 6 5 4 3 2 1

ACKNOWLEDGMENTS

Once again, I would like to thank my parents for always encouraging my creativity, and for believing in me. I am surrounded and supported in every way by my family: Forrest and Terry, Sharyn and Paul, Nancy and Gordon, My Bri-Guy and the two wonderful children he has given me!!I want to give special thanks to God for Chris and for Michelle—the editing angels He has put in my life. Without you...books would take twice as long to release and no one would want to read them anyway!

My coffee ladies—Annie, Libby, Linda, Pam, Paula, and Robin—you are as consistent and as bold as any good cup of Joe! I am so grateful for what we have together.

To Crossroads Church for always helping keep my eyes above the waves...

To Elk Creek Vineyards for an enticing, peaceful setting for writing.

Capturing Memories by Siobhan Eileen for headshots for my covers.

To Matt & Michelle for one of the kindest offers anyone could ever make...and then follow thru with...making my life easier through this season.

To Tami & Pat for providing the serene setting for the final touches of writing this book, as well as the friendship that lifts us up and grows each day.

To Dance Moms who pray in dark parking lots together—we now have our own dance!

I want to mention just a few of the people that have lifted me in other ways specifically during the time of writing this particular book, whether it be words, hugs, random texts, garage door checks, sunrises, or sending positive energy in their own special way: Dr. Morlie, Krista, Patty, Jenny, Larry, Suzannah, Jeff, Kim, Ken, Mary, Jenn, Teresa, Donald, Lisa, Jeremy, Sheila, and Rob Thomas.

"Hi, I'm Sunnie, and you are watching Sunny Side Up brought to you by Farm Fresh Egg Company, serving all continental states. Now you can enjoy farm fresh egg delivery to your doorstep! No matter where you are watching from this morning, you are never far from the farm!"

"Today, I will be talking to you about some more ways to improve your health, as part of the

BEST YOU series that we have been doing. So if you tuned in last week, you know that we spent a lot of time with segments on shopping for juicing, benefits of juicing, and recipes for juicing. So what happens after juicing? Today, I would like to show you some simple ways to make use of the pulp! Your juicer will separate the juice from the fiber for you. Naturally, you drink the juice, but did you know that you can use the pulp many ways, as well? There may be some nutrients left in the pulp, but most importantly, the pulp contains practically all of the fiber! The most common uses, well besides tossing it in a chicken coop," I wink, "are adding it to the broth for homemade soups or to the sauce to put over your pasta. Not only can you add fiber to your spaghetti, but you can bake this right into your lasagna or other pasta bakes as well. If you have a little more time, you can add the pulp to your baked goods for extra fiber treats. There are a lot of great recipes online. Last week I tried one for baking raw crackers using my juice pulp. I could have made them in a dehydrator," *No I couldn't, my dehydrator is a million miles away, suppose that I'm just lucky to have my juicer here in my new location,* "but I just used my oven on the lowest setting. I leave them on for about 12 hours until they were mostly dry, then cut them apart with my kitchen shears before baking them a little longer. If you want to really pulp-out in the kitchen, you could take your homemade crackers to a party with a veggie pulp cream cheese spread to top them! If you think that this all sounds great, but you just don't have time to use the pulp right away, keep in mind that you can store the extra pulp in the freezer until you are ready! Don't worry about losing some of the nutritional value; the fiber will remain! Oh and don't forget to be kind to your dog, pulp dog treats are easy and make a healthy treat for your doggie! I want to add that some veggies are toxic to dogs so please do your homework to avoiding using pulp with those vegetables. I hope that some of these ideas will work for you, so you don't have to throw the pulp to the chickens. Who has chickens these days, when you can get farm fresh eggs delivered to your doorstep? Thank you for watching Sunny Side Up."

"Cut," Robert calls out, "and a nice way to tie the slogan back in, Sunnie. Great work, team."

Sinking into the break room chair, I pull out my veggie pulp cranberry muffin to have with my hot cup of tea. I know that the segment went off well today, but I begin to wonder, as I often do, does anyone even use my tips? I dislike this feeling of doubting my information, and I never actually remember questioning my work back at home. Usually, I felt overly confident, as if anyone who didn't use my tips would be missing out of their chance for a sunny day. Something is really wrong with me. I am starting to doubt the importance of this fiber-packed muffin! I wonder if I could pull off adding pulp to red velvet cupcakes, remembering Mike mentioning one time that they were his favorite.

Taking another bite, I become completely aware of its texture in my mouth. *Okay, I am too aware of its texture in my mouth.*

"It's that bad, huh?" I hear from an unfamiliar voice pouring coffee by the counter.

"Wha— oh, no, it's fine actually," I say, looking up from my pulp muffin.

"Don't worry, Sunnie, I have no intention of outing you and suggesting that all of your great tips may not always, uh, translate," he smiles. "I'm Gregory," he suddenly reaches across the table to attempt to shake my hand.

Wiping crumbs off first, I finally offer up my hand. "Hi, Gregory. It's, uh, nice to meet you."

"No need to wipe so clean Sunnie, I am hoping to get some of the benefits of the...fiber," says Gregory rather coyly. It is not every day that Sunnie is so openly mocked. *Who is this guy? Or, more like, who does this guy think he is?*

"Actually, I believe you would have to ingest," I say.

"That's what she said! Ha!" Gregory laughs his way out with his coffee in hand.

Please tell me that did not just happen. I could cry. The only reason I don't is that I have another segment coming up with only a 5-minute make-up touch up. I remember all the times I had sat in the hair and make-up chair back at home with Sam reminding me not to cry and mess up my make-up. What I wouldn't do for someone familiar to walk in the break room, instead of a character like Gregory.

No such luck! I spend the rest of my break listening to two interns flirt in front of me like I am not even there. Only once do they ask me what my pulp muffins taste like, but the question hardly felt sincere. Before I have the chance to answer, the young female intern says that it smells gross from across the room. She continues talking of how she avoids food like that because she's so skinny that she cannot afford the slightest amount of bloating, or it would show on the camera.

"Don't you have another segment recording today, I wouldn't eat that if I were you," the female intern says before they walk out together laughing.

I trash the rest of my muffin. Not exactly because of the comment but because of it no longer tasting appealing. Nothing here seems appealing today. I need my sunny vibe. I cannot think this thought without thinking back to Mike. *Why can't there be a Mike at this studio?* Is it too much to ask for just one person to notice my color, my vibe, my feel, my...Mike?

I told myself for weeks that I wasn't going to think about Mike or what happened anymore. Thinking about it isn't going to bring the truth, I have moved on, and I am wiser for it. I learned my lesson. The next time a guy at work woos me into a situation where there are secret cameras, and passion, I will know better how to handle it. But that time I walked away. I closed the door, refusing to listen to his explanation for fear he would actually have one. Now I cannot really blame him that I don't have one! There is no explanation really that makes sense.

For me to suspect Mike, or Colleen, or anyone else following Alec's orders, will just leave me feeling paranoid, losing my ability to trust. At this point, I am smarter, but not jaded. It is better this way, coming here, starting all over. It is better! I am Sunnie, and I have something special to bring to any table or desk, I will not doubt myself.

All far away thoughts and self-talks are ended as I hear a voice calling my name. "Sunnie, I was just at hair and make-up, they are ready for you."

"Thanks. I was just about to go down," I say, not admitting to being lost in my thoughts. At least I didn't cry, though.

Walking down to hair and make-up I wonder who I will get today. I do miss Sam and the consistency. Stepping up to the next available station, I am mineral veiled by a face I do not know.

"You are a new face to me," my friendly attempt to start a little conversation.

"Your face is what matters, not mine," she says and continues to powder me. "All done."

"Thank you. See you later," attempting another friendly exchange.

"Uh-huh," she murmurs.

Not letting it rock me, I pep-talk my way to the studio. I am Sunnie; I belong here. I do add to this place, and to the world for that matter. New outfit from wardrobe, new topic for viewers—it's a new day—in TV world, anyway. Now let me appear well-rested and ready to begin my day, first thing.

"Hi, I'm Sunnie, and you are watching Sunny Side Up brought to you by Farm Fresh Egg Company, serving all continental states. Now you can enjoy farm fresh egg delivery to your doorstep! No matter where you are watching from this morning, you are never far from the farm!"

"Today, I would like to continue on our BEST YOU series, starting with your nose. Yes, you heard me, your nose. Your sense of smell is not only your strongest sense but also the one capable of affecting your brain activity! Now that is a powerful tool that can be used by anyone. Because of the clarifying and calming qualities, I like to cut a lemon early in the morning, taking in a whiff," I fake cut the lemon in front of me that is actually already cut, bring it to my nose, and take in a deep breath. "Nothing says good morning like the smell of lemon, well except coffee, right?" Winking directly into the camera, I remember discussing this with Mike in the break room one morning. I was on my lemon in warm water kick, and he said that I would be back to coffee with him in no time. He was right, about a lot. "So, uh, anyway," I pause collecting my thoughts. "Maybe I should have opted for coffee this afterno—. Morning! Maybe I should rely on my strongest sense and inhale the scent of cinnamon or peppermint to perk me up." *Wow, good recovery Sunnie girl may look like I meant to do that to make my point.* "Another easy pick-me-up is Rosemary, known for its stimulating properties; excellent to use in the morning. On the other extreme, what about when you need calmness? Lavender is my favorite in this category, but you may also like Jasmine for a calming effect." Breaking my rule of only allowing my mind to wander one time or less per 5-minute segment, I think about Jaz. I admit, I am home-station-sick. I will have to apply one of my other rules, and quickly to save this segment. When in times of no idea where to pick up, start with a personal story. "When I drive to work in my VW Beetle, I use the dashboard vase to my advantage. I put a stem of lavender in with my flower, so I can keep calm and drive on, without allowing the traffic jams get to me! *Ahhh, viewers love that. Make it personal for them in Alec Parker's voice runs through my head.* Picking up an empty essential oil bottle on the prop table by me, I take in a deep breath and smile to the camera. "Viewers, oh how I wish you could smell this jasmine for yourselves right now, I just know that it would uplift your spirits so that you would have a sunnier day! Thanks for tuning in."

"Cut. Nice recovery, Sunnie. These two-a-day segment filmings are confusing at first. Just think of it like this, your segment airs in the morning, so it's always morning," Robert says.

"Makes sense," I smile acknowledging how soft he has handled my lack of focus. He gives me a bit more understanding than I deserve so far.

"So when our Sunnie comes up, it's morning," Robert reiterates in his gentle corrective way with me again.

"Got it! Thanks," I smile back at his twinkling eyes.

"That was terrific, Sunnie, smell ya later, ha-ha! Get it?" Gregory approaches like we are great pals now.

"Unfortunately, I do uh, Greg—" I respond.

"It's Gregory. I bet you don't let people go around calling you Sun. Get it, like the sun? Ha! It's Gregory, a family name," he explains.

"Sorry Gregory, I was going to say Gregory actually, but you, um—"

"Okay Sun, wait for it, wait, EEEE," Gregory laughs, more than he should at his own joke. He is the only one laughing.

On that note, I walk out with a pasted on a fake smile, only wishing that Mike were here chasing me down in the hallway for two minutes of stimulating, arousing, and especially amusing conversation. Something much the opposite of the conversation I am experiencing here, especially the jokes, if that is what you call them.

A change of scenery could only help, so I pack up for the day. My place may not feel like home yet, but at least it is a space for me.

After dinner settled in my scarcely decorated apartment that the station provided for me during the transfer, I feel alone. Quickly I'm reminded that I don't have a flourishing herb garden just yet at this place. I should have just reached for my marjoram or frankincense essential oils, but instead, I log on to my computer. For the first time since my move, I do a search on some of the people from the station back at home. I probably should have stopped at the staff profiles with pictures, but I needed more, so that is when I became the stalker of my old life.

After I had looked at every single picture, I could find on the station's website I pulled up Google Images of any station events, zooming in on any frame that included Mike, and cursing anyone blocking him from my view. *Insa*ne, I know.

What is this? A picture of Sunnie Grey with her camera man, it reads below the box. Hastily clicking on the box, I attempt to open the picture above the description. *How could there be a picture of Mike and me?* We never took a picture together, not even a Selfie.

I close my eyes as the memory flashes right back to me in Mike's arms for our attempt at a Selfie atop the desk during our picnic. I remember the exact tone and chortle when he stopped posing for the Selfie to ask me more about a 'Helpie'. Nothing made me feel more special than the way he was always so thoroughly entertained by me. I had giggled explaining that I wanted him to use his left hand to push the button to snap the picture while I balanced my phone in my right hand. "It's a

'Helpie', get it?" I had explained. "See, sometimes with two people in the picture it is more balanced if a girl gets a little help...so I call it a 'Helpie'!" I will never forget the amused smile he wore at that moment, nor the kiss that followed as he whispered that he was willing to "help a girl out". The memorable kiss is the exact reason that we didn't remember to pose for the Selfie, or 'Helpie,' that I had wanted. Too bad there wasn't a fly on the wall with a camera to catch those moments.

I open my eyes quickly to an ironic thought. Careful what you wish for, there was a camera to capture our moments. I close the browser, as the picture with the caption has still not loaded. I should have shut the whole computer, but of course, I took a minute to look at my station's fan reviews.

Anytime I see my name, spelled right or wrong; I seem to have to take a peek. *I wish I didn't get on here at all!*

Beetmeup: Anyone catch Sunnie Grey's segment on pulp recipes?

Fitforfun38: I don't believe that she eats her pulp.

What does that even mean? Of all things on which to be questioned! Really? Really, people?

How could anyone accuse me of not eating my own pulp? To say it so publically is rudely inappropriate and to do it so anonymously seems cowardly! I do eat my own pulp! I do! And no one, I mean NO ONE is going to announce that I don't and get away with it! I know I promised myself and all of my family and friends back home and everyone at the station, including my bosses that I will NOT POST in response to people's comments, but this is too much. I do eat my own pulp and people are going to know that from now on!

Clicking on my status, I choose "eating" from the drop down. Not expecting pulp to be a choice, I begin typing it in and click enter before I over think it anymore. I smile proudly at my status update reading, "Sunnie Grey is eating pulp." There! I fixed this for all you doubters! But wait, I want credibility, and all I have is the truth to feel okay in these matters. *Oh no, what have I done?* I am not eating pulp right now; I only meant to address that I do eat my own pulp, not to lie to my people out there. How can I fix this? Make a pulpy snack, right now!

Instead of responding any further to these people that don't even deserve my response, I will make myself a snack, pour a glass of wine, and think this through for a while. This next line catches my eye before I could get up.

Trendygirlsgotguts: Sunnie is a trend-setter! I wanted to hate her, people, but beginning to think that it's not possible!

Gossipgirl4321: No doubt. At first, I thought this girl can't be real, but she is so consistent, I find myself believing what she says and does.

Says and DOES! Wow, could that be implying that I DO EAT MY PULP! Giggling out loud, I realize that I have forgotten to make a pulpy snack, and I actually could use something to eat.

Hangovertime2: I don't care if Sunnie eats her own pulp. She can EAT ME anytime.

Smoothiequeen: You are crude and uneducated Hangovertime2.

Hangovertime2: You don't know that. You only know I'm crude. You can EAT ME, Smoothiequeen!!

Smoothiequeen: You are right Hangovertime2. I just made an assumption that you were uneducated. My bad!

At least I get a giggle out of someone else's attacking drama while I scroll down to this:

DianaD: My sister was diagnosed with cancer last week. Her doctors suggested many dietary changes, including juicing. I have been at a loss for what to say to my sister, but we have been watching the "Sunny Side Up" Segment through this BEST YOU series and then talk on the phone with each other to discuss the topic. It has given us something to look forward to each day. I should mention that my sister and I are in different time zones, but we both DVR it and never miss. Maybe some of the tips are not the most important 5 minutes of everyone's day, but we have found them so helpful that I wanted to speak up here. Sunnie's ideas are welcome here. Sorry for the lengthy post!

Beetmeup: I thought it was an interesting topic.

Fastfoodfreefriend: Pulp is gross!

Cleancolongo#2: Don't knock it 'til ya try it Fastfoodfreefriend!!

Fastfoodfreefriend: I have tried it many different ways, and it tastes and smells gross. I eat healthily, but will continue to throw my pulp away.

Cleancolongo#2: Don't just throw it away Fastfoodfreefriend. If you don't have a pet or a garden, maybe a neighbor does.

Fastfoodfreefriend: I live in a high-rise apartment and work long days in the city. It is hard to keep up with juicing; I don't have time to worry about the pulp Cleancolongo#2.

Cleancolongo#2: Keep in mind that you can freeze it. Here is a link to the segment today about it, in case you missed it. Go to: www.sunnysideup.

Fastfoodfreefriend: I heard it. I know that you can freeze it, but I am not going to do anything with it so what's the point of freezing it?

Cleancolongo#2: In case you want to save up enough to use it later Fastfoodfreefriend.

Fastfoodfreefriend: Rather not use it later nor discuss it anymore now Cleancolongo#2.

Cleancolongo#2: No problem Fastfoodfreefriend. Check out my blog for links suggesting other ways to get more fiber www.fiberfilledfactsforyou in your day since you don't like pulp.

This is just too entertaining! Who would have thought that people could discuss pulp all day long! Who cares if I eat my pulp or don't eat my pulp, it just matters that people like talking about my pulp! ALL DAY LONG!

No longer am I tempted to search the comments made after the nose segment, not that nosey I decide. I have had enough of what other people think and would rather leave while still amused.

Hungry and giggly, I begin chopping broccoli with Veggie Tales songs playing in my head, missing my nieces and nephews back at home. Never thought homesickness would hit me this hard.

With homemade remedies for seemingly every sickness and ailment, I wonder what concoction I could juice for homesickness. I decide on grapes, already juiced and fermented.

"Hi, I'm Sunnie, and you are watching Sunny Side Up brought to you by Farm Fresh Egg Company, serving all continental states. Now you can enjoy farm fresh egg delivery to your doorstep! No matter where you are watching from this morning, you are never far from the farm!"

"Today, I would like to continue on our BEST YOU series," *Oh yeah...the best me, here in a jumper, with all of these thoughts running through my head, as I somehow give advice to the world out there.* "How does the way you feel about yesterday affect today? Well, I am going to tell you! At the end of each day, I like to reflect on what went well. This can look very similar to a morning pattern of identifying three things to be grateful for at the beginning of each day. For me, labeling three things that went well in my day, brings about a sense of calmness that makes for a really restless, excuse me, uh, RESTFUL—quite the opposite, night of sleep," tugging on the jumper straps a bit, unable to block the flashes of Mike's hands on my straps on the last jumper I wore. *I can only wonder how I am going to feel about this day at the end of the day; that is IF I get through it!* Thankfully, I remember the way I have been coached never to tug on my clothes while on the air. "At the end of the day, remembering and replaying parts that went well can be a tool for holding onto those good feelings. Plus, when doing this, who has time to obsess over any not-so-good parts of the day, right?" I wink, wondering if any of my viewers could possibly know how distracted and naked I feel standing here in front of the camera in a jumper-all-on. The jumper stays on, and the segment plays on, but all parts of my head other than my mouth, are with Mike. Only hoping that I have conveyed how powerful practices like these can be, I finally hear the word I have been waiting for: "Cut!"

No stops for me on the way to wardrobe; no one could have caught up to me, not even Mike if he were here trying. He is not. It is not as if I couldn't hear the constructive criticism regarding the clothes-tugging I had done on air; I just didn't want to wait one more minute to get out of there. Normally, I would, at least, give a polite nod to acknowledge that the critiques are accurate: I should always have any loose pieces taped in back, as to not distract me while on camera. I know this! I know all of this. My jumper straps weren't falling down; they were willed to fall by my deep, maddening attempt to replay his hand all over me again! How's that for replaying the good parts of your day? I can replay it over after all of this time, just like it was yesterday!

"So what did you mean this morning when you said that I would look cute in the jumper?" I blurt out, asking Sandy as soon as she comes to the wardrobe counter.

"Woah, Sunnie! I think that I meant that you would look cute in this jumper," Sandy responds. "And you do, by the way," she adds.

"Well, it sounded like you may have meant more than that," I watch for the slightest changes in her face. But the only one I see is frustration, with me.

"I don't know what else it could have meant, but I am willing to listen to what you thought I meant," Sandy leans on the counter, hands holding up her chin like she has all day.

"I, well, I have a history with jumpers," I say, in the first moment that I have felt at home here in this particular wardrobe room. I miss wardrobe Jazzy and her witty comments. Instead, I get wardrobe Sandy playing on her phone when I am trying to talk to her.

"A history with jumpers, as in HIS...STORY with your jumpers?" Sandy says, turning her phone around and filling the whole screen with a picture of Mike and me at the fireworks.

"Where did you get this?" I asked in shock that I had never seen a picture of us together before.

"You're funny, Sunnie! Really? It's not hard," Sandy laughs while swiping to the next one, even closer up.

"How do you have all these pictures of me...with Mike?" I ask, sounding a bit freaked out.

"Everybody does, Sunnie! You haven't seen these?"

"I didn't even know they existed," feeling foolish and impatient, realizing that I had been so close to seeing this when the picture hadn't loaded correctly. Instead, I had given up, closing it instead of getting to view it on my own, rented space.

"Don't you ever google yourself, Sunnie?" Sandy asks like I have four heads.

"I never thought to," I say tampering off and turning to leave. I may as well see them on my own device in my own dressing room.

"Sunnie, did I upset you? I just assumed that you knew. Do you want to talk about it? We could grab a drink after work tonight if you want?" she asks seeming entirely sincere.

"Can I let you know later, Sandy? I just want to go to my dressing room for now," I say.

"Sure! You know where to find me!" Sandy says with a smile.

Staring at pictures of myself, Mike, and the jumper on my own phone in the privacy of my own dressing room, the tears fall silently, until I release a few sounds that I couldn't help letting slip out. Private around here means thin partition walls with no sound barrier. Privacy, in general, doesn't seem to have much value today! The looks that I am giving Mike in some of the pictures were reactions for him at that moment, not for the world to see. I hadn't even seen them! You can't give that look to the mirror.

Picture after picture, hand in hand, and then there it is—lips on lips. It looked way sexier here than what it was. I remember how overwhelmed I was in the instant that we talked about the Sabbath. He was like no other man I had ever met and THAT is what I sealed with a kiss.

Part of me wishes that he was the boyfriend that he looks like in the picture. We seem totally unaware of anyone around us, yet people captured these images all the way down the street. More than wishing that he was my boyfriend, I wish these were my photos and not just public images that I searched for on the internet. I concentrate on the pictures only without clicking anything, to avoid reading a word of people's comments. Just seeing us together was enough pain for one afternoon.

Maybe I should have kept the jumper for sentimental reasons instead of mailing it back to the station anonymously. No, I don't need it, I have one million pictures surfacing to remind me.

The jumper does look great, actually. I hope the one I wore in this morning's segment was as cute on camera.

"Sunnie, are you ready for make-up?" I hear from outside my dressing room. *Oh no!* I forgot about the filming the second segment this afternoon.

"I need make-up." All of it.

"What am I supposed to do with your face?" asks the make-up artist.

"I'm sorry. I, uh, I got bad news," I say.

"Well, I got some more for you...you will not look good on camera with those puffy, tear-stained eyes!" says the make-up artist, with no trace of empathy.

What have I done? I stare at the mess in the mirror.

"Never mind. I have an idea. No make-up necessary for this segment! I just 'woke up'," I say quickly before fleeing from the chair and back to my dressing room to gather a few things.

Arriving directly to the set, stripped of my made-up look, out of breath, and in my plush white robe, the heads turned.

"Sunnie, why aren't you ready? You are on in two!" Robert asks in his set-manager voice.

"I am ready. I promise I am ready for this," I say with faux-like confidence.

Greg smiles hugely. "But are we ready? I saw a video on the internet of her...taking off layers. I bet we are in for a real treat today!" Gregory's library voice is equivalent to most people's conversational voice and with his evident excitement, came off more like some people's rock concert voice. Everyone heard it.

"I am right here," I smile in his direction. The room remains quiet other than a few nervous chortles. "Look, I am just changing segments; it will still fit in the BEST YOU series. I have wanted to write something like this anyway."

"As in...write it, turn it in by your deadline, obtain full review and approval, then prepare for the segment?" Robert asks.

"Not exactly, but I know this can work if you can just grant me a little freedom here today. I won't let anyone down," I plea.

"But Sunnie, you know this is not how we do things here. Every segment needs to be approved, to avoid simple disasters that could...easily be avoided. You're not just local anymore," Robert explained.

"That's right little Dorothy, you're not in Kansas anymore, hahaha," Gregory chimes in thinking he is so funny that if he adds a few ha-ha's to his comment that everyone will join in. Not happening!

Ignoring Gregory's side show and only addressing the boss, I say, "Please. Please trust me with this."

"Oh Sunnie, how can I say no to pouty red lips protruding from a very white face...let's see what you got. Give me two seconds to get approval from my boss," he walks away from me with his cell phone to his ear, and literally seconds later he is off the phone with a big smile directing everyone into place.

"Do you need any props?" he asks in a hurry.

"No, I brought my cucumber slices from my lunch. I may use this chair here," I say, still loading in my head what I may do.

"Hi, I'm Sunnie, and you are watching Sunny Side Up brought to you by Farm Fresh Egg Company, serving all continental states. Now you can enjoy farm fresh egg delivery to your doorstep! No matter where you are watching from this morning, you are never far from the farm!"

"Today, I would like to continue on our BEST YOU series. You may be thinking, 'Wow Sunnie, this is not your best look', but we all know...it's a process, right?" I smile with my white masked face directly into the camera, amused that I pulled this off in the time I had. From weepy, make-up stained face to this fresh face mask look in an instant. *How could this not have been planned?*

"Yes, it's a process. Today, I am going to show you some very simple ways to improve your skin with ingredients you probably have on hand. For today, I have made a quick and simple mask from dry milk and honey. There are so many easy-to-make-masks with ingredients like turmeric, mint, apple-cider vinegar, just to name a few. But I like this particular mask because of its simplicity."

"It is not really science...I just added dry milk powder to a small bowl of warm water until it was a thin, pasty consistency. Then a few drops of honey to mix in. I like to add the honey last, after the dry milk is dissolved into the warm water, to avoid getting clumps. Some other added bonuses to this recipe, one, it smells nice when applying to your face, and two, you can make a convenient substitution without having to run to the store. If you don't have dry milk, you can substitute coffee creamer! You could even do this one in your break room at work, people! Well, that is—if—you are in a work environment conducive to walking around with a mask like this on your face," winking into the camera, I notice the smiles and head nods from some of the crew. "If I were at home, I would be able to walk around, multi-tasking while this mask dried. But sometimes I like to relax while I'm masked, adding a scented candle, filling the room with my favorite essential oils diffusing. Maybe add some sweet music or sounds of nature, waves crashing...you get the idea." Easing down into the chair, as if it were my home-spa setting rather than an office chair on the set, I continue, "With these effects, you might like to set up a warm foot bath to relax you while you sit. And now for my favorite part, no more puffy eyes, a cucumber can be your best friend. Place a cucumber slice on each eye and restore peaceful thoughts while the natural elements of this unique veggie can restore your tired, puffy area surrounding your eyes." With eyes covered, head tilted back instead of facing the camera, in my sincerest, almost therapeutic voice, I say, "It doesn't matter what made you cry, what kept you up through the night, or any other reason for the swollen, tired eyes. It only matters that you can fix it...on the outside...and perhaps on the inside as well. Thanks for tuning in today. I hope you try the mask and will soon wash it off for a fresh face, ready to face anything."

"Cut. Fantastic work, Sunnie. Really...you are amazing," calls out Robert in front of everyone.

Overwhelmed by the enthusiasm in his compliment and relief that the unpracticed, impromptu segment played out perfectly, I throw my arms around him without thinking it through, "Thank you for trusting me."

"Oh, uh, sure, Sunnie. Of course," he hugged me back until we both realize that my mask is now a white cloud-like spot on the shoulder of his dark suit.

"I'm sorry. So sorry, I was just excited, and I sort of forgot about the mask and didn't mean to, uh, leave a cloud of white...on you," I say, feeling silly.

"It's okay. They'll be able to get it out, I think. And until then I have a little Sunnie cloud on my shoulder. I'm proud of you Sunnie. You're everything a—that everyone told me about you." There was a strangeness in his delivery of the compliment that I couldn't ask a follow-up to because of Gregory's interrupting lack of humor.

"Don't you mean a GREY cloud? Get it, Sunnie Grey?" laughs Gregory.

I get it. Forgive me if I don't laugh, might have heard a lot of the name jokes by now," I say excusing myself from the room.

Managing to hold back some more tears until I reach my dressing room, I admit to the masked girl in the mirror...I miss Mike. As soon as I heard another of Gregory's silly name jokes that I have heard my whole life, I flashback to the old station. I remember like it was yesterday Mike saying, "You will have to tell me how you got your stage name next time," before he had briskly walked away.

Every single time I walk off the set, I miss Mike chasing down the hall to steal two minutes with me. *What I wouldn't give for one.*

That's it! I will follow-up to that conversation from just after I met him, I will share with him the stories of my name. It will give us closure—the kind we never had.

Practicing all the way home of how I would start the conversation was useless in the end.

"Hello, Mike's phone," said the clearly female voice on the other end.

"Sorry. I think I have the wrong number."

"If you are trying to reach Mike for video work, he is away for the next few days. You may want to try back early next week if this isn't urgent," she offers.

"No, not urgent. Not at all. I have a wrong number. I am actually trying to reach a different Mike, I mean, person. Thank you!" I hang up as soon as I shut-up. Uhhhhhh...a different Mike? Yeah...like one waiting on me. Not this one with a woman answering his phone.

My hurt and surprise turn to anger as the evening goes on. I'm mad at myself for not trying sooner to get to the truth, but since it is easier to be mad at him, I will assume that the truth is that he did try to film me for money, for job advancement, for pleasure, for whatever. He is not an innocent victim of someone else at the station's doing. Nope! He is guilty, and now he is off somewhere doing his video thing to the next girl. I just know.

Good thing I didn't get ahold of him and tell him some silly story about my name, like it, were old times. How humiliating that would have been. This way he has no idea that I called and of course, I will NEVER do it again. I would rather stay mad at him forever!

I should have spent my energy calling Jaz, or some of the other girls. I should have called anyone but Mike. *Why hasn't anyone attempted to contact me? Doesn't anyone miss me? Doesn't anyone wonder how I am doing? Should I have sent a note along with the jumper?* There has been so much hype about my jumper-all-on-jumper-all-off, first at the station and then in the media; it has almost taken on a life of its own! Out of sight out of mind, Sunnie-girl is part of the past I suppose. But as for the jumper, who knows?

~

Meanwhile back at the home station...

"Do you know anything about this?" Tom, from the delivery room, asks at the wardrobe counter.

"Looks like a package to me!" Jazzy says quickly and right back to work.

Pulling the item out a little further, Tom states, "It's a jumper actually or so I have been told. Dan, in the ordering department, says that it's a brand we sampled, but for some reason, this one has arrived with just one size. Dan said that is unusual," Tom delivers raising his eyebrows to display his best detective face.

"Let me see that!" Jaz pulls the jumper from the mailing package to get a look, "Oh my god! Uh, it's just...a jumper. I will handle this. Thanks."

"Why the huge reaction at first?" Tom asks.

"Oh nothing," Jaz lies.

"It sounded like something!" replies Tom right away.

"It is just so cute, I have really been wanting a jumper like that one, but in my size, ya know? Anyway, back to work, many wardrobe orders to fill!" Jazzy ran to the back with the package in hand, thinking that the sink room should work as a very private office for a minute.

Once she is sure that she is alone, Jaz begins to investigate the package. "Well, well...jumper-all-off and here at the station doorstep! Sunnie, what happened? Did you take this jumper-all-off or did he? Are all these rumors flying around true? Is that why you haven't contacted anyone? So where could this jumper-all-off have turned up to be sent and returned to the station? Oh Sunnie Girl, what have you done? Interrupted by a knock on the door, Jaz jumps.

"Jaz, are you alright in there?" asks Pat.

"Yes, just thought that I could just get a tiny little powder off of this, um—shirt, off of this shirt, and not have to send it out to the cleaners. I think it is needed right away, so I'm, uh, doing my best," Jaz lies to Pat through the door.

Sounding like Sunnie, with all of the cover-up and impromptu thoughts, Jaz realizes how much she misses the girl! Jaz never thought she would act like her too!

Another knock at the door quite soon after the first one causes Jaz to startle again. "Pat said you were acting funny so I knew that could only mean one thing, you are up to something. Let me in, Jaz, or I will scream and draw a lot of attention to whatever it is you are doing in there," calls Anna. "Jaz?"

Jaz lets out a squeal of frustration that is entirely misread.

"Oh my, Jazzy, you are not alone. I will keep watch! Sorry to have bothered you, sweetie," says Anna.

"Oh for goodness sake, get in here, hurry, shut the door!" says Jaz grabbing Anna quickly and attempting to close the door again.

"No way! With you and your—?"

"There is no one in here with me, you idiot, I just didn't want you to know what I was doing! But you wouldn't go away!" Jaz yells in a whisper.

"But you wouldn't let me in, or open the door to explain, and then I heard some strange noises, did I not?"

"You did, yes, but there is no one in here with me," Jaz repeats.

"Ohhhhhhhhhhhhhh. Okay. I 'm not judging," Anna states.

"Oh my god, there is nothing to judge, my noises were just noises of frustration."

"O—kay!"

"Never mind, just help me here!" Jaz begs.

"Okay!"

"Look what arrived at the station today. Remember this piece?"

"Remember it? Well, that jumper-all-off went down in history! Practically made its own debut in the video, huh?" laughs Anna.

"No kidding," says Jaz under her breath, followed by, "So what do we do with it?"

"Why are you asking me?" asks Anna.

"Because you are the only one else that knows about it!" whispering at the top of her lungs, Jaz delivers.

"Well, I only know about it because you pulled me in here."

"I let you in here when you wouldn't just mind your own business!" Jaz snaps.

"Hey, really, why did you...let me in?" Anna asks.

"Oh because you were so sweet to try to cover for me when you thought that I had someone in here. That's a friend! Right then I knew I could trust you with this," Jaz admits.

"So at least I am a trustworthy idiot friend? Nice!" Anna suggests.

"Oh never mind, what are we going to do with this jumper?"

"Where does it have powder on it anyway?" Anna asks

"It doesn't have powder on it!" Jaz whisper-yells again.

"But Pat said that you stated that you were back here trying to get powder off—"

Jaz cuts her off, "I was just trying to suggest a reason why I would be in the sink room, to buy some time, but you were so persistent, and I didn't want to have you out there drawing more attention to the situation. Do you understand now?"

"Yes, now I do. I am your persistent, trustworthy idiot friend," Anna jokes.

"I'm sorry, Anna. I am pretty stressed about this. I just don't want any more drama for Sunnie, you know," Jaz says.

"Jaz, she is not coming back. I've seen this all before, and it goes the same all the time. A girl gets discovered...she's off to Hollywood...she is the IT girl for a while...her popularity tanks...she re-invents...she soars...she's a joke in the media...she makes desperate career choices...she further tanks...she disappears until her episode of 'Where Are They Now?' runs on television."

"Are you finished? You know Sunnie was different, right?"

"I know Jazzy. I know. I miss her too." Anna leans in for a hug and Jaz accepts, knowing that Sunnie would want it that way.

In the midst of the friendly embrace, the sink room door swings open wide by a hand on the handle—the hand belonging to Pat, who is furious that she is running wardrobe all by herself since Jaz and Anna have been hidden in the closet.

"You two are—, okay, not judging, nope not judging. I just could use a little help out here," says Pat, walking away shaking her head.

"Just a friendly hug," Anna calls out.

"Oh, my. Just let her think whatever she wants. We don't need anyone else in on our secret."

"Our secret?" asks Anna.

"The jumper, you idiot, I'm sorry! I'm still tense," Jaz snapped.

"Of course. Hey Jaz, I will slip it into my personal bag for now, until we figure it out."

"Good idea."

In walks Colleen straight for the counter as Jaz returns to duty, "Hey Jazzy, what's going on? I came to see if you guys needed help since there are lots of complaints around the station about a back-up in wardrobe."

"No, we're fine. It was just...it was just really busy for a stretch. It's all good," Jaz states, wondering if she should share with Colleen.

"What did you do with the jumper?" Colleen asks.

"Oh, you know about the jumper?" Jaz asks, a bit stunned but trying to keep cool.

"Tom told me that it came in the deliveries. He asked me what to do with it, wondering if he should bug Mr. Parker with it since it had no note, so I just sent him to you with it," Colleen admits.

"Oh yeah, no problem. I'll take care of it," Jaz says.

"Just so that you do right away. We are lucky that no one sold out, releasing it to the tabloids or something crazy. I wonder how it found its way back here anyway...too bad it didn't come with a note from the person who found it. Oh well. Maybe it has something to do with why Sunnie asked never to be contacted by anyone here at the station," Colleen comments.

"Wait—do you really believe that Sunnie said that?" Jaz asks, jumping on the opportunity since no one ever brings up the fact that it didn't really sound like Sunnie at all.

"Yes, she told us with certainty. Well not to me, to Mr. Parker. He took her very seriously. That's why he sent out a note to everyone on staff to honor her request or lose their job, so to speak," Colleen explains.

"That is pretty serious; I'd say," Jaz replies, still wondering what could have possibly happened that night in the jumper.

Interrupted by Anna coming through to leave at the end of her shift, the Sunnie conversation ends.

"So, uh, I'm taking off for the day...but you could, you know, uh, stop by later, um, if you want. We could, yeah. Just call me later, k?"

"Sure," Jaz says in front of Colleen since she couldn't ask if Anna still had the jumper in her bag nor ask her why she had to act so weird!

Jaz knew it was coming by the look on Colleen's face as Anna awkwardly flew out the door. "What is going on with you two? Is this a new thing?" Colleen asks.

"Nothing."

"Like the nothing that goes on behind closed doors in little back rooms, nothing?"

"Not what you think, Colleen, really," Jaz remains calm.

"It's none of my business. Oh, I just don't want to hear it if Mr. Parker finds out." Colleen starts laughing.

"He can't discriminate!" Jaz reacts abruptly, which makes no sense even to herself.

"I know, what I meant is that he has fantasies about that kind of thing," Colleen laughs right up until the next question that Jaz asks.

"And he tells you these fantasies?"

"Well, uh, okay I better get going. You are busy here," Colleen realizes that she slipped, admitting knowing Mr. Parker exceptionally well.

Not until after Colleen left this time, in her own puddle of uncomfortableness, does Jaz process that she never made it clear that there was truly nothing between her and Anna. *Why can't Sunnie be here? She would know how to handle this. She always knows how to put a positive spin on things.* Jaz finishes her shift with thoughts of Sunnie and with wondering why Sunnie wouldn't want to be contacted by anyone at the station, even her friends. There has got to be something more to this, but Jaz fears she will never know the truth.

Several "sunnie-style" attempts to write new segments for the next deadline fail miserably until I give up on working from home for a while and head to a Pilate's class. *I need a break, I need exercise, I need peace, and most of all I need some inspiration. If I'm being honest, I need a reason to justify wearing these yoga pants all day long!*

The two-segment-filming days are completely worth it to have these days in between when I do not have to go into the station. A nice break. And when I say break, I do mean a fun bun and stretchy clothing!

Some exercise will also help block the should-I-or-shouldn't-I battle that keeps weighing heavily on my mind regarding my dinner invite: co-workers meeting on the day off to have a meal together. Apparently there is a different type of food each time, this time being Chinese. The urge to be around people is delightfully welcomed, but then I recall that they are new people, not that there is anything wrong with that. I just miss...familiar people. Of course, I had felt this same way when I started at the last station, after leaving my comfy, cozy job where everyone seemed to be a "Sunnie fan", encouraging me and my silly ideas until I landed a job sharing those ideas with an audience. Look at me now; sharing my sunny ideas with the nation—well, at least the part of the nation that tunes into the "Sunny Side Up" Segment!

Sharing my ideas and faced with sharing dinner too? This is too much. No wonder I cannot write new segments; my mind is not clear. I am listening to too many voices that my own is unable to speak, even to me. Even though I haven't been able to make it to these classes for weeks, I am still able to align my body properly again. What about my mind? I have leaped right into this new station and new life. With all of the excitement and going through the motions, where am I in all of this? *Where is Sunnie?* Well, besides...on a mat, in a gym, behind perfect asses in obscenely tight leggings, while balancing body weight with up-side-down boobs pouring out the top of a sports bra? I am very aware of where I am, thank you! I am the one down here at the foothills, concentrating on breathing despite the mountains of dense breast tissue!

Thank God for the instructor's words, reminding everyone not to try to look around the room since it could be dangerous for the neck. "Keep the neck straight and only gaze upward" never sounded so good. I look upward, alright! I look to Him—the one with the power to keep me breathing during this minor boob-alanche!

When I get out of this class, I will get in my car and blast a song that can put me back in my place faster than if I put the pedal all the way to the floor,

"Remind me who I am." I need this because I am pretty sure that I am the type of girl who can share dinner with new people. I know that I am and that I will benefit from it. People are all different, which I thrive on, always a fan of letting people float their own boats. It seems the quirkier the personality, the more fascinated I become. I can float in a similar boat, rather than jump ship when someone or something seems a little odd. "So whatcha going to do with your Sabbath?" Mike's voice plays through my head instantly, which could bring me to my knees if they weren't flipped over my head at the moment. I cannot look around for Mike right now without breaking the rules, and my neck. Besides, I know it came from inside my head because there is nothing auditory coming through with the gentle knee squeeze of this pose, exactly why I like it. Hip alignment over shoulders is all worth it for the chance to momentarily cut off any aural distractions! If only I could block the internal sounds.

My intense thoughts carry me through my class with little or no attention to those around me, until the end when I realize that the same few ladies are looking at me again as they did upon my arrival. Grabbing a towel from my bag, I wipe my head then place the towel around my neck as they still seem to be staring at me. Rather than experiencing anything more awkward than this I smile toward them. "That was a good class, just what I needed. I'm Sunnie." I reach out my hand.

"Oh, we thought that was you," the first one says, while the two other ladies become busy rolling up their mats.

"You watch my segment?" I ask, excitedly. God forbid I think I have a fan in this town.

"No, but I saw you on something online—a video of you stripping on-air...in your hometown, I think. Whatever it takes to get ahead, I guess. You just used what you've got, right?" says a woman that I have no idea how to take.

"Wow, oh, well...let's not take that out of context," I say with a nervous giggle.

No one else laughs.

"Okay, well...have a great day," I say smiling quickly, then exiting.

Gripping the steering wheel without starting the car, I whine out loud repeating her words, "WHATEVER IT TAKES TO GET AHEAD?"

Really? All of that clearing my head and my senses, and then this? Breathe in, breathe out, meet toxin and converse with her. What had I planned to do when I got back to my car? I cannot remember after that conversation! Finally, and angrily, I start the engine and begin the race home. Why bother with the radio, my loud thoughts play for me above any sound. Then I remember, push play, and sing, allowing Him to remind me who I am. "In the loneliest places...can't remember what grace is...tell me once again...who I am to you," I sing, knowing that He may have to keep telling me. At least I know who to ask!

The road race home that started in the act of anger ended in the rush to write. What had started with writer's block, soon changed to numerous new new segments flowing faster than I could get into my apartment to type them.

Hours later, I practice my new segment in the mirror just for fun.

"Hi, I'm Sunnie, and you are watching Sunny Side Up brought to you by Farm Fresh Egg Company, serving all continental states. Now you can enjoy farm fresh egg delivery to your doorstep! No matter where you are watching from this morning, you are never very far from the farm!" Today, I would like to talk to you about what fills your tank. You may think you have heard this concept other ways, like whatever floats your boat, whatever fills your bucket, whatever keeps your cookie from crumbling, but I want to call it 'tank' for today's purposes, for a plethora of reasons.

Interrupted by the beeping of a new text message, I pick up my phone to find, "Hey Sunnie. We are moving to the fortune cookie part of the dinner, and we haven't seen you yet. You are not just late, right? Are you not coming? Hope all is okay."

Uh-Oh! Dinner—Chinese dinner! Oooooopps!

I reply right away, "Sorry, I should have let you know, but I lost track of time."

"No problem. Everyone was just hoping to get to know you better. Next time!"

"For sure!" I text, hoping that I do mean it.

"One more thing...we picked a cookie for you. It is perfect for you, Sunnie!"

Before I can text Sandy back, the phone rings in my hand. *How can I not pick up? She knows that I am not busy!*

"Hello," I say.

"Let me just read it to you, Sunnie. It will be easier. Your fortune reads, 'You have the power to write your own fortune.'

Of course, they can't see or hear my smile, but it's huge.

"Can you hear me, Sunnie? Isn't that perfect?" Sandy asks, excitedly.

"Just perfect. It couldn't be more perfect actually!" I admit.

"We all thought so. We were talking about that if you were here you would be re-writing everyone's fortunes to say something even more positive," Sandy jokes.

"Well, I don't know about that, but I do have a game I like to do with fortunes. One of my—"

"Hold on—. Hey, Sunnie. There, I put you on speaker. Guys, listen up. Sunnie has a game with the fortunes," she calls out before I have a chance to back out.

Hearing all the hellos through the phone, I begin with, "Hi there, uh…I was just saying that one of my professors in college used to tell us always to add 'in bed' to the end of every fortune. Given that we are all co-workers, we could add 'at work,' maybe? I don't know."

"In bed is fine with me, Sunnie," a male voice calls out.

"Who said that?" I ask with a slightly nervous giggle.

"Ahhhww Sunnie...what you don't recognize my voice...in bed?" the same voice calls through the again as everyone else laughs.

"Nick! I don't think that you are supposed to add 'in bed' to everything just to the end of the fortunes," Sandy corrects.

"Actually, you don't need to add that at all. I said 'at work,' Nick," I say, acknowledging that I know who I am talking to now.

"Thank you for the clarification...in bed, Sunnie," Nick says, making everyone laugh, including me.

"AT WORK...at work!" I say loudly into the phone hearing the giddiness in my voice.

"Okay, Sunnie. At work too then!" Nick calls back. *Wow...are we really flirting like this on speaker phone in front of everyone when he has barely even spoken to me at work? I am not even exactly sure what he does.*

To re-direct the conversation, I ask, "Can you read mine again and add 'at work' to the end?"

"Sure, Sunnie. Let me find it again. Oh, here it is. It says, 'You have the power to write your own fortune...at work'," she says.

"I like that!" I say.

"Here's mine, 'Soon life will become more interesting...at work'. That's even better now, huh?" She says with lots of laughter, and some oohs and ahhs in the background.

"Okay, here's Lori's fortune, 'The harder you work, the luckier you get...at work.' So true, ha-

ha!" More laughter from all. *Who knew a speaker phone conversation could be so much fun?*

"Wait, listen to mine," calls out another voice that I didn't recognize. I couldn't hear all of it before the next person was reading his. Hysterical laughter caused me to laugh along, but I really couldn't catch half of it through the phone with all of the commotions.

Finally, there's a small break in the chatter for me to ask, "How many people in the restaurant can hear all of this?"

"We're the only ones left in here, drinking Tsingtao!" she says.

"Well, have fun guys. I'll see you all...at work," I say, wrapping it up.

"Wait Sunnie, you didn't hear mine yet," says Nick.

I smile so big that I am glad none of my co-workers can see me through the phone. "Okay, let's have it, Nick."

"You will wait in bed for someone new...at work," Nick delivers.

"Oooooooooooooooooooooooooooooh," echoes loudly through the phone from all, while I say nothing.

"Aren't you going to say anything Sunnie? It was...your game idea, right?" Nick asks.

"Good luck with your, uh...wait, Nick," I say.

"Thanks, Sunnie. See, you're not the only one who can write your own fortune," Nick says, cockily.

"Whatever fills your tank, Nick. Which reminds me...I need to get back to a segment of that topic. That's what I was writing when you called," I say. "Good night, everyone. Get home safely!"

"Good night, Sunnie," I hear over and over before I push the button to end the call. Hmmm, that was an unexpected event.

I pick up where I left off practicing my new segment.

"Only one outfit today Sunnie, the big staff meeting replaces the afternoon filming for everyone," Sandy says, handing me over the clothes.

"I forgot about the meeting!" I say discouraged.

"It's okay. It's not until this afternoon," Sandy adds, and walks back over to the counter, handing someone else clothing.

"I know, but...I have a problem. This is what I wore today. I didn't bring anything professional for the big meeting," I whisper.

Looking at my bare-shouldered-strapless-sundress look, Sandy smiles and says, "You certainly did forget. I will try not to take things personally."

"Personally? What does my unprofessional sundress have to do with you?" I am confused.

"Nothing. Nothing at all really. But it will when I replace it with something you can wear to the meeting," Sandy smiles.

"Really?" I look around to make sure no one is listening. "Thank you! I owe you!" I say smiling.

"Yeah sure. Maybe you could buy me a drink sometime," Sandy laughs.

"Yeah, okay," I didn't know what else to say. The way Sandy had laughed when she said that, I wasn't sure exactly what she meant.

"Sunnie, I was only teasing about the drink. I will get you an outfit for the meeting."

"I don't mind the drink!" I say.

"Well I won't hold my breath based on last time when you were a no-show," Sandy says.

"Oh...that. I'm sorry. I did forget to let you know I was not up for a happy hour the other day. I left out of here pretty fast after my last segment," I explain.

"It is no problem. Why don't you go out with Lori and me, and some of the girls for a while this weekend? You don't know anyone here in town, do you? You must need people to do stuff with?" Sandy asked, obviously wondering what I do all weekend.

"Oh, yeah, I don't really know anyone, yet. I will take you up on the offer, soon," I say smiling.

"I'll hold you to it! And about the outfit, I can't promise what it will be, but I will avoid jumpers since you have a history with them," she laughs.

I just smile, realizing that I may have underestimated Sandy, all because she wasn't Jaz. Her "his-story" wordplay comments are pretty witty, and she wants to go out and talk, like friends. I guess I may need to give the place a real try, instead of worrying about who and what I am missing back at home.

Putting my own thoughts on hold for now, I re-direct my attention to what Sandy is quietly telling me. I must get focused for this big meeting. I don't say a word and just listen to her instructions. Sounds like she has done meetings like these plenty of times.

Gliding into the hair and make-up chair, I ask, "So what is the big deal about these staff meetings, like later today."

"For starters, usually big changes follow," the make-up person says.

"Big changes?" I ask.

"Yes, usually based on the ratings."

"Ratings are everything, I suppose," I state, thinking to what happened to me at the last station.

"That's where the money is...always looking for the new 'it' to give the viewers what they want."

"The new 'it'?" I ask though I know what she means, I hadn't experienced it as much here.

"You'll see. Things move faster here than probably what you are used to. Enjoy it while you're 'it'!" she said with an attitude.

"Interesting perspective," I say, digesting this and trying to find a way to leave her with a sunnier perspective.

"Before you know it, you're done!" she says spinning around and gesturing with her hand to get out of the chair.

"Well then! I guess it is crucial to make the most of the time!" I say while hopping down with an extra bit of spring to my movement. If my positive, chipper spirit didn't at least make her wonder how I do it, after the depressing plan she attempted to project on me, then she can worry about "it", alone. I have a job to do and for now, I'm doing it—on and off the camera! A positive attitude can be contagious. Maybe she will catch this one.

Isn't anyone around here noticing my vibe? I don't mean to continue to think of Mike and smile, but he did always notice my vibe. A little positive thinking in that direction couldn't hurt, I suppose. It feels right and improves my sunniness.

Before I head to my dressing room, I go straight to the director's office to ask if I can change the segment for today. Then he will know that I did hear him that when I need to make a change, I must consult with someone, not just show up at film time with the wrong look for the segment! Plus, it is not like I am asking to wing it like I did the other day. This time, I only want to pull from an existing, approved segment that I had previously written. I just have to be convincing that I have a gut feeling that this is what we at the station, and our viewers at home, need today. This is "IT"!

Knocking on the door with a brass nameplate reading, "Robert Kline", I hear the "Come in" and take a deep breath.

Not as I anticipated, but may work in my favor, all of the set directors that I work with are in Robert's office.

"Hello, Mr. Kline and everyone," I say cheerfully. "Sorry to interrupt your meeting, I just wanted to ask a question regarding today's segment."

"Ask away," says Robert, smirking at me addressing him so formally.

"I would like to request to change my segment for today. I am positively sure that we need something positive and, um, up—"

"Sunnie, the ratings suggest that people love this BEST YOU segment, let's just stick to what we have for today," Robert says. Looking down at the schedule in front of him he continues, "Yes, about the great uses for improving and tightening skin with Apple Cider Vinegar. People love to improve their looks. These ways to help the viewer enhance their looks are it, Sunnie!"

"I agree," says Mr. Williams.

"Me too," pipes in Mr. Carl right away.

"Also Sunnie, we all have a lot going on with all the big shots flying in this afternoon for the meeting. Let's keep everything else simple, honey, okay? You understand, right?"

Nearly saying yes because I do understand, but feeling so passionate about this, I respond boldly, "Actually, I think people that worry mostly about their looks need to know that they would look a whole lot nicer with a smile on their face! No one is smiling today, Mr. Kline. Everyone is saving it for later—for when the big shots come, I suppose? Thanks for hearing me out, though. Positivity is contagious by the way," I turn to leave, with a smile anyway.

"Sunnie, if it is that important to you, and it is a piece that is already approved, we could check with the boss and see."

"Oh, she will love it! Thank you, Mr. Kline!" I say excitedly.

"I meant him, the boss above her, but yes I think he will go for it as well," Robert says, shaking his head with an amused smile shared by all in the room as they look back at me.

"Don't be late to the set. I will let you know only if he has a problem with it. Otherwise it's a go. But keep in mind it must be impressive because he and all the big shots will be here later today," Robert adds.

"You won't regret this. I know it is about the ratings and the viewers, but maybe you can catch more viewers with sunshine, than vinegar! I am so happy!"

"Well, like you say it's contagious. Hope that it works for people at home too," he says smiling.

I wish I had time to analyze what just happened in there. I am all for expecting a positive outcome, but it seems that they treat me with kid gloves and always let me have my way. For today, I will just be happy that they do!

"Hi, I'm Sunnie, and you are watching Sunny Side Up brought to you by Farm Fresh Egg Company, serving all continental states. Now you can enjoy farm fresh egg delivery to your doorstep! No matter where you are watching from this morning, you are never far from the farm!" I know that I should not make any changes to my script since I already pushed it a little by changing the topic for today. I cannot help myself, I thought of a better intro!

"How's everybody doing out there today?" I say, keeping the balance between enthusiastic welcome and an opening band at a rock concert. "I know today is going to be a great day! I can hardly wait to see what is ahead of me after this segment. Do you wake up with this feeling—the feeling that something good is about to happen? Well, maybe you should...because something could!"

"As part of the BEST YOU series we have been doing, today we are going to be talking about positivity. For the BEST YOU—we cannot underestimate the power of our positive thoughts! I'm sure you could even pick up on my positive vibe and body language, right from the beginning of this segment. It's attractive, right? Well sure it is. It is a proven fact that we are drawn to positive people. Why is this? It is because those people are 'up-lifters', right?" I intentionally make big quote marks in front of myself with a huge, bright smile. "Another reason may be that positive attitudes are contagious! Keep in mind that so are negative ones. You have to be deliberate about which ones you catch!"

"Here are some ways you can do just that. It starts with your thoughts. I'm sure you have all heard the glass half empty vs. glass half full scenarios. Do you naturally see a glass half full? The feeling is incredible if you do!" I hope my tone of voice comes off as sincere; it is hard to contain the excitement that a positive attitude brings. "If it does not come naturally then you have to train yourself to do so. But guess what? It will positively be worth it! Simply begin with your self-talk, by not allowing yourself any negative messages. Keep it positive until you have a brain half full of it! You cannot just say that you are positive, it has to start with those positive thoughts, positive feelings, and positive actions. Allow your mind to think that anything can happen. IF you think of your mind as a room, you can let negativity shade it and make your mind dark, or you can choose to open the windows and let the light in the room to illuminate your mind," I slow everything down a bit to make sure that I am read as sincere. I'm extremely grateful for this job as an outlet to affect others! With one more positive smile, I begin to deliver a choice for the viewers. "If positive and negative are different directions, which way are you going to go?"

"Cut. Nice. Nice work," calls out Robert.

"It's obvious which direction I'm going; I think that I like to follow the sun actually," a familiar voice calling out from the back of the room.

"Mike!" I say, willing my legs to move from my frozen, stunned position. "You're...here," is all that I can say before my whole body is wrapped around him. The power of positive thinking!

"Oh, Sun. I have missed you," Mike whispers close to my cheek.

"Mike...you have no idea," I say sweetly, not letting go. "What are you doing here?"

"I think you may know," he says, gently picking me up while still hugging.

For the very first time in history, Mike and I walk out at the same time, instead of him chasing me all for a two-minute talk.

"Wait here. I will be quick. I just have to change out of these clothes, drop them off to wardrobe, and I'll meet you back in this room. Help yourself, there's tea and coffee and—"

"Sun, I think this break room is pretty similar to any break room, go do what you need to do," Mike smiles.

With a little fear that this is all a dream and that I may return to the break room to find him gone, I talk myself through it all the way to the dressing room. *Oh Sunnie girl, no negative thinking! Especially not when something this great just happened, Mike is here! Mike is really here.* Changing back into my strapless sundress, I remember that I have one more thing to handle—something appropriate to wear to the meeting!

Where is she? I say to myself, running into the room to drop my clothes and pick up what Sandy has ready for me. Cutting through the others lined up at the wardrobe counter, I grab the jacket on the end of the counter from where Sandy left it for me and smiled as I politely push through. I am not impatient, but I'm in a hurry, which they would all understand exactly why if they saw what was waiting for me in the break room.

Jacket folded over my arm; I practically skip to the break room to find Mike. I find a lot more! *Really?* Every person in the building with boobs is surrounding him.

"Uh, I'm back. Want to go outside?" I say toward Mike over the top of anyone in between.

"Outside? Oh yeah, sure. I forgot that it's warm here. I came straight off the plane," Mike says.

"It's warm. And Sunny," I smile as if we are already alone. I am so happy that he is here.

"Aren't you worried about the ramifications of all this public hand-holding?" Mike says as we are finally out of earshot from everyone, walking out of the building.

"I didn't even think of that, actually. But you flew out here, showed up at my studio on the opposite coast, all for me—people are already talking!" I say as I lean in for another rest in his strong arms.

"I'm glad I'm here with you, Sun, but I need to tell you some things," Mike says, rubbing my arms and back.

"Sure. I need to tell you some things too," I suggest playfully. I should want to ASK him some things, but none of it seems to matter right now.

"Sunnie, listen. There are some things you need to know. Things you need to hear from me—"

"Mike, there are some things you need to know, like that you cannot talk in that tone, and be this close to my face and expect me to take you seriously—oh...Mi," smothered in his kiss, I stop talking. Pushed up against the wall of the building kissing, I don't care what he has to say. I feel positive that we can work through it. Whatever happened back in that studio that night could be explained. He came all the way here for me, and that is all I need to know.

"I'm sorry, Sunnie," Mike says loosening his grip.

"Sorry that you are not kissing me all of the sudden?" I ask.

"I didn't mean to react like that. I thought I could just talk to you, uh, first. But maybe, maybe I am the one who cannot stand that close to you."

"It was both of us, Mike," I confirm, for what it matters.

"Still, Sun...there's more you need to know before that happens again," Mike says very seriously.

"Are you married?" I ask quickly.

"No!" Mike protests.

"Are you engaged to be married?"

"No, Sunnie," Mike answers.

"Do you want to get married?" I follow with a giggle, "I'm teasing, Mike. You just seem tense."

"C'm 'ere," Mike murmurs, taking me in his arms again.

"Wait, aren't you afraid that we will attack each other again?"

"We're going to be okay, Sunnie, but we do need to talk, now," still in his serious voice, Mike holds onto me, without letting go of his tension.

"Give us this minute, Mike," I rub both of my hands down and back up, feeling his firm muscular build along with the knots.

Mike breaks our silence for apparently what can't wait, "Sunnie; there is a lot you don't know about the—"

"Sunnie, it's time for the meeting," a voice calls from the door, causing us both to jump like we are busted teenagers.

"Oh, oh my, I lost track of time." No doubt! "I'm sorry, Mike. We will talk later, okay? I have to go, but I'm so glad you are here!" I hold the sides of his face and give him a quick kiss before I grab the jacket and begin dressing myself in the hallway on the way to the meeting.

I have my professional look in place before I take my seat in the room. Would have been nice to catch a look in the mirror, but what I did catch is a positive attitude, and I feel confident that this jacket rocks on me. No one will even know about my little slip in forgetting the meeting and lacking in a professional look! I will have this jacket returned to wardrobe before anyone knows of my illegal borrowing of the station's clothing for my own benefit. Perfect!

Without even thinking I grab my lipstick out of my pocket and dab it on discretely to the lips that had just been kissed, then returning it. Wait— strange thought, I didn't put lipstick in the jacket pocket. I had planned on going back to my dressing room before the meeting to freshen up. Did Sandy really think of everything? If so, that girl is good! Maybe she is more like Jaz than I realized. I wish that I didn't agree to go out with her tonight, though. Of course, now that Mike is here, she will understand, I hope.

The room is starting to fill in more. I smile and wave hello to a few people across the room so that I don't appear too lost in my thoughts. All I can think now is: let's get this meeting going, people, I happen to have a hot date waiting.

Quiet, nervous chatter is broken by Lori, a wardrobe girl, bursting in, appearing in somewhat of a panic. "Has anyone seen Mrs. Dennison's jacket? She is our guest speaker today." The room is quiet enough to hear the jacket liner rub against its owner's skin, but no one claims knowing anything about it. "It's black. It has some detailed trim on the sleeves that matches the suit skirt she already has on for the meeting. Wow, you people are quiet. It's not as if she thinks someone stole it," Lori laughs, alone. "Okay, so no one knows anything about it? She last had it in the conference room and thought that maybe someone may have picked it up, maybe dropping it off to wardrobe or something."

Looking down to the pen in my hand, I notice a shiny black trim on my sleeve that I hadn't noticed when I put the jacket on while my eyes were still adjusting to being outside. No, it couldn't be!

Everyone stands and turns toward the door to the back of us, as the big shots begin walking in. Among the nice suits that I had only seen on Mr. Parker, back in the day, it is hard not to notice the one without a jacket. Straining my neck from my seat as she goes by, I have definitely figured out on my own who Mrs. Dennison, our guest speaker is, and I have also figured out that I am wearing her jacket. How did this happen, to me?

I play back in my head my conversation with Sandy this afternoon. I hear her saying, "I will leave a jacket for you Sunnie, but when you come in for it don't ask anyone anything. We can get in so much trouble for this sort of thing. People used to abuse this and clothes would...walk away. You won't need a whole outfit, just add the jacket to your dress and it will be fine. You and the other on-cams will be to the left side when you walk in, and all of us behind-the-scenes staff will be in the right section or the back section. There will be a single row of chairs down the left side facing in where you and the other talents sit and obviously all the bigwigs will then take the seats in front of the whole group. Take a seat early and then just stay seated for the meeting and you will look as professional as anyone. She was right about that! I'm sitting here in a designer jacket already sprayed with expensive perfume! I remember thinking it was strange that something from wardrobe would have a scent like that, but of course, I questioned nothing so that I wouldn't get anyone in trouble. *Who's in trouble now? ME! Oh my, I have even used her lipstick!*

Mingling is winding down, and seats are being occupied. What can I do to avoid a very embarrassing situation—not be seen wearing someone else's missing jacket, for starters! In a very smooth action, most likely acquired from all the times of taking on and off jackets in front of the camera for my segments, I slip the jacket off my shoulders, down my arms, and onto the back of my chair as I lower myself down to a seated position. I would have loved to have slipped it on someone else's chair, far from me, but this was a better option than wearing it during the meeting.

Realizing that I'm completely missing the introductions, I will myself and my bare shoulders to sit up tall and focus, just in time for the introduction ceremony that will change everything. An all too familiar voice begins greeting the crowd, "Hello everyone. It is so nice to be here, and to see all of your faces in person today." *You have got to be kidding me! Why would they invite him? This is my new start. I no longer need his approval. I'm a big girl, and that's why I left that environment to come here. Why is he here?*

Not feeling so much like a big girl when I hear him call out my name, as the sound of hands hitting together barely drown out the pounding of my heart.

More than just my shoulders are naked in this room. One look from Alec, motioning me to join him in front of everyone, strips me bare. He knows his power over me, and how far he can push me, though his control over me wasn't enough to keep me. I am Sunnie, I rise.

At least I felt that I had risen above the situation by leaving when I did and starting fresh, under a female boss, nonetheless. Staying true to myself here at this station no matter how difficult it has been to go against what is expected of me. Has that really been difficult? It seems that whenever I need to adjust my path, a new one to my liking, is designed for me. Paved in front of my eyes, my new path, with no obstacles. How many times have I heard, "Let me check with the boss" followed by a, "YES, Sunnie." Clearly, because my IDEAS were good, right? Right? It has to be my ideas, and not Mr. Alec Parker, right? The Mr. Alec Parker is waiting for me to join him!

Except for the weights in my feet and Super Glue apparently connecting my entire sundress to the chair, I rise to the occasion quite smoothly. Obviously, his magnetic force, which seems to control the sun, will be enough to draw my body toward him once again, not to mention that a hundred others are waiting to see what happens are expecting me to.

Confidently walking up to the front of the room, only because there is no other way I would walk than confidently, I join Alec in a public handshake that I thought would never end. With a plastered smile, I shake hands with each member of the board lined up while every professional in the room continues to clap for the girl in the yellow strapless sundress. I never worried less about my professionalism; it is more than obvious now that I am the IT girl. It matters not. What I wear becomes the IT outfit. I wouldn't be surprised if I turned around and found everyone losing her jacket, purposefully. Further confirmation comes from the side of me when Mrs. Dennison leans in to thank me for making her feel so comfortable, after losing her jacket. She laughs whispering that the stuffy, board room look is so over-rated. Did I just say, "I know, right" to my boss? Her smile is friendly, rather than disapproving. My sunny, down-to-earth disposition works again. This is IT.

The clapping and chatter halt as Mr. Parker speaks again, "Our Sunnie," gesturing toward me to his right. "This is going well? Right?" he greets the crowd again, this time with a rhetorical question. I can't help being giddy by the response, rather than embarrassed.

"This was one ray of light that I just couldn't keep to myself at the local station!" Alec declares with a huge grin. *Wait, what? I left. I did that! What is he talking about?* "I have to tell you, though, this is proof that you cannot contain light in a box and just get it out when you need to illuminate the room, or a city, or the whole country for that matter." Turning his body toward me and resting his hand on my shoulder in front of everyone, Alec continues, "Miss Grey, you are the real deal. Viewers love you. We all love you. You were much too big to keep hidden in the small town scene. America needed this kind of sunrise!" The clapping starts up again, and might as well be slapping me on one cheek and then the other. The strangest feeling occurs to accept this kind of acknowledgment while processing what Alec's role has been in all of this. Scanning the crowd, no one seems shocked or surprised by Alec's words. *Does everyone else already know that he is the master behind everything here? Am I the last to know? I thought that I had left him, not aided in his plan. I am nobody's puppet!*

Alec adjusts his hand but never removing it from me during the entire time that he speaks my praises. Of course, to everyone out there it looks professional—as professional as one can pull-off on a bare shoulder in front of a mixed crowd.

Yanking my puppet strings, Alec pulls me against him right in front of the entire room full of eyes, while whispering during the embrace, "You are MY sunshine, Sunnie. I have truly missed this."

Back in his business voice, Mr. Parker begins aloud, "We'll let Sunnie take her seat again; we have a lot to cover today."

Not really sure what was covered today, I walk out briskly at the end of the meeting to avoid talking to anyone until I process.

Of course, there is no time to process anything other than why Alec has barged directly into my dressing room. "Sunnie, I've missed you," he starts. "Though I have been able to keep tabs and watch from a distance, I want to be more involved again."

"Alec, really? I just had to find out in front of a room full of people that you were still involved at all! Imagine my surprise when I had thought all this time that I had moved on, that I was the one to do what was best for me, that I was the one to take risks. I picked up my life and went for it, Alec! Little did I know that you had picked me up and delicately placed me back in a new scene like I was just some little sunshine icon game piece? Roll the dice, Alec, see how many spots you would like to move me forward or back this time!" I didn't start out shouting, but I had really never been so misled that I got carried away. With a deep breath, I calm myself back down to say in a broken voice, "I was a fool—your fool."

"Well Sunnie, if not me you would have been someone else's fool," Alec says, in his typical, arrogant way.

"What does that even mean, you think I am not strong, not smart enough to control my own life, my own career?"

"I do Sunnie, but you are also young and a bit gree—"

"Are you kidding me? You can't just say that you are sorry? You have to show me that you know best...because I am young, and inexperienced, and would fall for anything? Is that what you think?" I want to cry but will not give him the satisfaction nor chance that I may end up crying on his shoulder.

"I don't think you would fall for anything, Sunnie, but it seemed like you were about to fall for a particular cameraman—one who did not deserve your trust nor your time and attention."

"Oh, and who did deserve my trust, my time, and my attention Alec? You?" I feel sick.

"You can't trust him, Sunnie. There are things you don't know," Alec says calmly.

"Why should I believe you?" I ask.

"Sunnie, you were already out-growing the local station, everyone knew it. I couldn't have kept you there, so I helped you go," Alec explains and believes himself.

"Dishonestly," I quickly throw out.

"So the way I handled it wasn't as, uh, upfront, as I would have liked, but I had this little girl in front of me stomping her feet and—."

I cut him off right there, "Alec—there you go again. That is not how it happened. I stood up for myself. I drew a line, one that you kept crossing, and then I would find myself slipping back under your spell. I left. It was not a little school girl throwing a tantrum; it was an adult decision. I have a mind of my own, and I wanted to try to use it."

"Come 'ere, Sunnie. I know that you have a mind of your own, that's what I love about you. I honestly tried to help you get out there in the world, be big, be yourself," he says, again sincerely believing himself and moving closer to rub my arms and back and anything else in his reach, all to comfort ME of course. "I just couldn't let you keep yourself from the world for some hometown relationship with someone on the crew who didn't deserve you."

Startled by the quick knock, Alec and I both freeze before I begin to open the dressing room door. Oh, my, who knows what he just overheard.

"Sorry to interrupt. Mr. Parker," Mike nods. "Sunnie and I have some unfinished business before I take off," Mike says from the doorway.

"You're taking off? I thought...I don't know what I thought. I cannot breathe." Not waiting for a response, I barrel past Mike and practically run through the door to the exit. Stopping in the stairwell, I no longer hold back the tears.

I cannot lose Mike again, but I cannot turn to him either. *Did he know all along that Alec was behind my re-location? Did he play along? Is he a puppet too?*

The screech of the stairwell door pulls me from my thoughts. Fearful to open my eyes to see if it will be Mike or Alec, I am startled to see that it is neither. "Sandy? What are you doing out here?" I ask.

"I think I should be the one asking that," Sandy says. "But I think I know."

"You have no idea," I say tearing up again.

"Sunnie, I have some idea now. I went to your dressing room to let you know that the jacket incident all shook out, and no one knows anything involving you. Little did I know that the jacket escapade was the least of the scandals of the day involving you! Wow, Sunnie, what do you do to these men?"

"These men?" I ask.

"I overheard Mr. Parker talking to that guy that came here for you. You know—the gorgeous one, with the body that—"

"Yes, I know. It's Mike. Go on. What did you hear?" I ask.

"It got pretty heated. Sunnie, Mr. Parker is not to be disobeyed. He is a powerful man," Sandy says with concern as if I don't have a clue.

"I think I pretty well know that Sandy," I say.

"Well, I think your friend Mike thought that he knew that too before today, but you should have seen how shocked he was when Alec had him escorted out."

"Wait. He what?" I asked, hoping that I did not hear her right.

"He called security and announced to all those gawking in the hallway that he would not have Sunnie being stalked by this man. He told the guard that this was not the first time and that he had seen him back at the other station following you," Sandy continued.

"That's not true! Well, not entirely true. It was mutual, Sandy. Mike never did anything like—" I pause to flashback to the night with the camera, struggling to catch my paranoid thoughts flying around.

"What about your mutual thing with Alec? Sunnie, just admit it, I heard everything," Sandy confronts.

"There is nothing mutual about Alec and me! I feel like a naïve schoolgirl, even a puppet at times," I say, not sure why I am offering Sandy more information.

"So you are saying that you don't love Alec?" she asks.

"Love? Are you kidding me? I don't even know how to love. And Alec? C'mon. He doesn't know love; he knows power," I say with disgust.

"Sunnie, I am sure this is hard, and maybe you don't want to admit it, but I overheard Alec tell your friend Mike the whole story. He made it clear that you two were trying to keep the relationship a secret and out of the press. He told him that is why he sent you here until it blew over. When Mike accused Alec of deliberately putting space between you and Mike, Alec laughed and told Mike that was only what you wanted Mike to think. I could tell Mike was hurt to hear it, Sunnie, but he deserved to know," Sandy said, attempting to comfort me.

"He didn't need to hear that Sandy because it is not true!" I yelled, echoing in the stairwell.

"Sunnie, is it true that there is a sex tape out there of you and Mike? It sure sounded like both of your men knew about it," Sandy states boldly.

"No, well yes, they both probably know, but no. It's not exactly a sex tape!" I say horrified, forgetting to control my volume.

"*Not exactly* never goes over well in the media," Sandy says.

"You have to believe me...there is no sex tape. There may be a really hot foreplay tape floating around, but there was no sex," I say, defending myself.

"Mike clearly said that the film was so dark that no one could prove that it was you. Then Alec countered with the argument that it was so dark that no one could be sure that it wasn't you."

"My gosh, Sandy, how long did you listen to them argue?" I ask.

"None of us could pull away from it. I am sorry, Sunnie. It was really juicy when it was happening before we figured out it was happening to you," Sandy attempts to touch my shoulder, but I resist.

"Sandy, who's WE? How many people heard this?" I ask, dreading the answer.

"I have no idea Sunnie. I was the only one at first, but the hallway was full by the time Mike was escorted out," Sandy admits.

"Oh my—I," I stop to process that not once in all of these months had I ever fathomed the idea of an edited video that made the act continue further.

"What are you thinking, Sunnie?" Sandy asks sincerely.

"I am thinking that I never set out to be a celebrity making tabloids, and I certainly never thought I would have a stunt double, especially not one caught in the act. I cannot open my eyes for fear there is a mirror," I say with my eyes tight shut.

"Sunnie, you are the most real, believable girl I have ever known. People will believe you no matter what they think they see."

"And that has usually worked for people in the media, eh?" I ask rhetorically.

"Listen Sunnie, if Mike just does what Alec told him to do, the tape will never surface. Alec said himself that he wanted to protect you from it as well. He stated that they were actually on the same side on this one," Sandy says as if it is a comfort.

"What the——. Please tell me what he asked Mike to do!" I unintentionally raise my voice, again.

"It was simple, Sunnie, just to stay away from you as he had been doing. He can keep his job and everything. He will be fine, Sunnie. He is a great looking, well-spoken man. I mean at least when he is keeping his cool, he is," Sandy says as if there was more.

"Just say it, Sandy. Did Mike lose his cool when security came?" I ask, dreading her answer once again.

"Oh no. He was smiling. No force necessary, the guard just walked along side of him to the door. The escort out seemed mostly as an act to appease Mr. Parker actually."

"So why did you suggest that Mike had lost his cool?" I ask.

"Well, when I first peeked in on them it may have looked worse than it was. Mr. Parker was very close to Mike's face, let's just say...describing what your body does for him. Mike instantly picked Mr. Parker up and shoved him against the wall, defending you for every word Mr. Parker had said.

Then Mike calmly let Mr. Parker back down to the ground saying all this stuff about how he trusted that you would see through a man like Mr. Parker all on your own. He said that the very fact that Mr. Parker did not give you enough credit would be the exact reason that he could never have a woman like you, to begin with. The way Mike went on and on about how you are such a strong and smart woman, not just the naïve little girl that Mr. Parker wants to keep to himself, was kind of hot if I must say," Sandy says smiling while repeating all that she had heard.

"So is that it?" I ask, just wanting a different ending than that of Mike being escorted out of the building and out of my life.

"Oh, he said one other really hot thing, which had all of us girls melting," she said, biting her bottom lip and shaking her head as she remembered.

"Oh yeah?" I dare to ask.

"Oh yeah. He got right in Mr. Parker's face, lifted him off the ground again in one motion and said that he had no worries of you seeing through him. Very confidently, Mike told him that in all the time that Mr. Parker spends wanting to see himself as the one in charge that there is a higher power, bigger than either of them, that gives...now let me get this right for you, Sunnie, because it was such a powerful line. Mike was like, 'There is a higher power, bigger than you, giving Sunnie her light'. Then he told him something like, 'You will be the one left in the dark—that is...unless you finally seek light from a different source than you have in the past'. I have never heard a man talk like that. Then he calmly put Mr. Parker down on the ground again.

"Sounds like Mike. And unfortunately, that sounds like Alec also," I say.

"So you really don't have a secret relationship with Mr. Parker—Alec, you say?" Sandy grins as if she busted me and wanted more of the scoop.

"Not in the way he is presenting, but yes, I can now see that I have let too much go on in secret. I can explain, but not here. I think I will take you up on that drink after work. Is it okay if it is just you and me, though, I don't really know Lori that well for this kind of a story?" I ask.

"Sure. Listen, we better get back in there," Sandy adds.

"Give me just a couple moments to just breathe here before I have to face all of the faces inside if you know what I mean. Could you do me a favor? I know it's a lot to ask but could you find out if Alec left the building yet and text me?" I ask desperately.

"Sure, but I don't think he will leave until he gets what he wants," Sandy delivers with a smile.

"He will never get what he wants, that I do know," I say confidently.

"Well, that makes one of you. You might need to clue him in!" Sandy laughs and gives me a quick hug. I honestly could have held on to her longer.

When Sandy is barely through the door, it begins to open again, and I hear a voice say, "May I enter your temporary office? There has been a line waiting to talk to you."

What? A line? This is crazy. Can't a girl just hang out in the stairwell sometimes?

"Sure, come in," I say because I don't know what else to say.

"Sunnie. I am flying out this evening, but I wanted a chance to tell you that you have left such an impression on me," says Mrs. Dennison.

"I bet!" I say assuming I know what she means and that the whole world knows about Alec and me, and what actually isn't happening. *Oh and then there's that sex tape with Mike floating around too!*

"Sunnie, you need to hear this. I doubted you. When Alec called and told me that I had to take you on, I heard of your age, saw your face and assumed you would be the next Alec-chosen-IT-girl whether we liked it or not. I used to get upset. I used to try to fight him back. I used to attempt to prove him wrong, but I am worn down over the years by his dog-cat chasing behaviors and promises that it is just business with a new fresh face. I learned the hard way," Mrs. Dennison says sadly.

"I am not trying to pry, and it's none of my business, but it sounds like you know Alec well, or for a long time I mean," I ask hesitantly, hoping that I am not overstepping.

"Both—well and for a long time. It's okay. Ask away; it's really no secret. Alec has been with a lot of women who were trying to climb the ladder. I wasn't the first nor the last."

"Mrs. Dennison, thank you, but I'm not even sure what to ask."

"Sunnie, please, call me Annette," she insists.

"Oh, okay. Thanks. I will try. Honestly, it feels strange calling the head of the station by first name. I respect you as my boss," I say.

"Like it first did with Alec, felt strange? I know. Let me guess; he caught you behind closed doors, he initiated a professional-but-overly-friendly relationship but made you feel like it was your idea. As if that is the way you wanted, and even needed, it to be?" Annette laughs a bit.

"Something like that," I say. "You do know him well."

"Well, I should. Alec and I lived together for quite a while. Believe it or not, I was his IT girl for a spell. I was 15 years younger and light years more naïve. I hadn't made very many decisions in life, but then again, I didn't have to with Alec. Making decisions for people is his specialty. I remember feeling so lucky to have him to do so. So basically he hired me, built me, moved me, and left me!" Annette laughed again, but I could tell she didn't think it was funny.

"Oh it makes sense actually. He measures himself by man."

"More like by young women, honey!" Annette smiles.

"Oh I know, but what I mean is that Alec has all the talent and money and prestige in the world, but he only measures himself with worldly treasures. If he always has the next bright shiny thing on his arm, he believes that he's IT. He needs these IT girls to make him feel like IT.

"That's IT, Sunnie. You really get him! He's a dog, isn't he?" Annette says smiling again.

"Not necessarily...a dog, but..."

"Oh c'mon, don't tell me you have learned all of this and still have a soft spot for the man?"

"Call it a soft spot, call it naivety, call it whatever you want, but what it is is: simply having the ability to see redeemable qualities! Alec can be better than all of this." I have even surprised myself with the epiphany. "Alec Parker can be better?" Annette questions.

"Yes, anyone can."

"But you even acknowledged that Alec uses his power and charm to get whatever he wants. He sure couldn't do that any better! Geez, the man is the best at getting what he wants!"

We sit in silence for a few more moments before Annette turns to me very seriously to ask a question. "What do you want, Sunnie? I can tell you don't want Alec, and I am pretty sure you don't even want this job, with strings attached as they have been."

"I want—" my voice breaks, I tear up, and I finally continue to speak, "—to brighten the world." I get it out first, then process how silly it must have sounded.

"That, Sunnie, is exactly what you are doing," Annette smiles and puts her arm around me.

We sit in the stairwell in silence, both teary-eyed, unprofessionally dressed professionals. I respect her no less in a silky tank without a designer suit jacket, calling her by her first name, nor by finding out that she only said yes to me all those times because she was ordered to do so by Alec. She seems to respect me too. I knew I was going to like having a woman boss after all, even if only for a short time.

No knock, just an impatient man coming through the door to stare at us. Alec speaks to Annette only at first. "Nette, honey, can you give me a few minutes with Sunnie? She has had a rough day."

"Oh and let me guess, you are the perfect person to comfort her?" Annette says with a different tone than she used during any of our talks.

"C'mon Nette, jealousy never looked good on you before. Go freshen up and we can go get some drinks before I fly out," Alec offers.

"Really? You think I want drinks, this time, Alec? I have actually had enough with your surprise visits," Annette says, with hurt in her voice. I remember back to the other station when I saw Colleen's reaction to seeing Alec kiss me for the first time. All these women, hurt.

"Actually, drinks, that sounds nice! I would like to treat you, Annette. You have been good to me in my time here," I say, already knowing that Alec's head would nearly pop off that I know Annette on a first name basis. *Who is holding puppet strings now Mr. Parker?*

"Well, on second thought, that does sound nice! That is...if Alec here can handle two strong women at once," Annette sounded so confident. Beautiful moment! Alec looks very uncomfortable as he begins, "It's not that. I just…" Alec stuttered, for the first time.

"Actually Alec. I cannot make it after all. I have a boyfriend to locate. I think you know who I may be talking about," I say with a smile, knowing that it would irritate him. Alec knows that he can rub against someone, deliver a very sexy kiss, even lure some women to his bed; but being someone's boyfriend isn't going to work until he stops throwing his power around. "I'll leave you two to sort it out!"

Rushing to my car, desperately hoping that Mike waited around in the parking lot after being escorted from the building, I am disappointed to find no gorgeous man in sight. Would he have had a rental car? I didn't even think to ask how he got here; I just remember him saying that he came straight from the airport to find me. I could not have asked more questions earlier due to all of the kissing!

Trying not to take this personally, but so discouraged that he didn't wait for me, I walk to my car to find no note, other than the pranking kind someone did with their finger in the dust to remind me to wash my car. I never let my car get that dirty, but the other evening when I couldn't get ahold of Mike, I parked on the beach because I just needed to do something that I couldn't do at home. I had to turn it all off somehow when no other simple steps to happiness were working.

I know what Sandy had said about Alec threatening Mike to stay away from me, but I still thought we would talk it out, especially when she told about how calmly Mike left, with confidence that I would eventually see through Alec's ways.

Once I leave this parking lot, I honestly have no idea where to look. He doesn't have his cell phone with him. I know my brilliant, witty Mike, and he would not just leave without a sign.

That's it! I stop the car, throw it in park and fling my door open. Once outside I read the side of the car again, "Wash me@thecarwash." *I hope I am right!*

Zooming across the street to the car wash on the corner, I never saw a finer car wash attendant! I pull in and roll down my window.

"Other side, Sunnie," Mike points to the passenger side, so naturally, I start to roll down that window also. "No, honey, unlock the door."

"Oh!" I giggle as Mike gets in the passenger seat.

"Let's go through the automatic wash. I could use some air-conditioning too. I am not used to your weather out here, Sunnie. It was a long wait out here for you."

"Oh okay, I will turn the air on and put the windows up then," I say as I pull into the automatic car wash lane.

"You are going to need to put the windows up anyway, silly girl, right?" Mike jokes.

"Oh yeah, of course," I hope he doesn't expect me to think right now. I am still processing how a plan like this one has actually worked.

"I was banned from the station parking lot too when they found me hovering around your car waiting for you," Mike explained. "I don't think your buddy Alec will find us in here.

I put the car in neutral and Mike reminded me not to bump anything. There was absolutely no talking inside the car wash. Intense, wet, sloppy kissing and hair pulling. We held on to each other as if driving over a waterfall, instead of a simple carwash. Our first truly private moment yet.

"Want to go again?" Mike asks.

I pulled around and back into the same lane without speaking a 'yes' out loud. Four car washes later, we have a bright shiny car and bright shiny faces.

"Now that we are, uh...clean, let's go somewhere that we can talk," Mike says smiling.

"That is IF I remember how to drive and not rely on a track to pull me forward!" I tease, but I am kind of serious.

I pull into a park right down the road where we sit on top of a picnic table and begin to talk.

"Sunnie, I do forgive you for not contacting me, but just for the record there were reasons why I could not contact you," Mike explains.

"Mike, I called but someone answered your phone and said you were out of town."

"Well I was. I left my phone so Alec wouldn't locate me. I came to find you. I wanted to tell you that he was behind your re-location position before you were blind-sided by him again."

"Wait. You came to warn me. I'm sorry how I jumped you, Mike. I thought that you came to see me, kiss me...and get back to—"

"Sunnie, believe me I came for all of those things," Mike says convincingly. "Then your affection was more than I could handle. After so long of wanting you and no way to make it happen. I had so much to tell you before you went into that meeting, I tried Sunnie. I am so sorry that I wasn't successful in warning you. And unfortunately there's more, Sunnie, way more."

"I heard there is a video of us that looks pretty real," I say.

"You know about that? Sunnie, I had nothing to do with the editing, I promise. Alec has been holding it over me to keep me from contacting you."

"I'm sure he has," I say. "But, Mike, what did happen? I cannot forget about the night of the fireworks...that call you got from Colleen telling you that—"

"Sunnie, I can explain. I don't know for sure what Alec had worked out that Colleen was trying to warn me about, but I am guessing it was finding out that you had accepted the re-location position. He probably figured that it would drive us apart and that he would see you again in the future. Maybe he thought that by then you would be grateful that he had a hand in your new position."

"But that doesn't explain why Colleen thought you were in on it somehow?" I ask, confronting him.

"I still don't know for sure, Sunnie, but I promise you almost everyone was thought to be in on it. When you were leaving, Mr. Parker sent orders to reward the career of anyone who could convince you just to cool off and return to the station by Monday. In the media he didn't want it to look like anything more than you having a day off or something simple like that. Then all of the sudden, it was no problem and all worked out, but that didn't change anything for our night as far I was concerned. Sunnie, you have to know that was not the reason that I planned the picnic night for us.

I told you then, I needed more than two minute talks with you."

"Mike, it's so much. I believe you, but I have believed some of the untruths for so long now that my brain is having trouble catching up," I say.

"I know. I do," Mike says, inhaling a deep breath. "But while we are getting all of this out in the open anyway, why didn't you tell me that you were planning to re-locate so quickly? Sunnie, you could have told me the truth."

Ignoring the hurt in his voice and obviously simplifying the situation, I answer, "It was on my mind, but I didn't want to ruin the little time we had left together."

"You didn't give me the chance to use the little time we had left together to make a plan. I am not trying to get off the hook here Sunnie, but I wasn't the only one to not trust in what we were starting, you know, to really give it a fair chance."

I sit silently. I know that he is right.

"You didn't trust me that I was acting of my own will and not following any of Mr. Parker's orders that night, including the attempt to get you involved in some video scandal for power over you later!" Mike sounds so disgusted.

"I always knew in my heart that you would not have made a video to blackmail me, I just couldn't figure out why when I had noticed the camera light that you didn't react more...I don't know...like jump up and get to the bottom of it...I don't know..." I say in a whining voice when it is the last way I want to sound.

"Okay. You got me. I now know that I should have, but Sunnie, at the risk of sounding weak, or whatever, I was only reacting to you, your body, your skin....if I am being completely honest, Sunnie, it was all I cared about at that moment. It wasn't until later, after you ran out, that I realized that there had been cameras on us. I frantically tried deleting all of the footage from the computer, but it was too late. All files were transferred to the other studio before you had even cleared the building. I received an anonymous call right away telling me to have no contact with you or the video would be the end of your career. I certainly couldn't see how at the time because you and I both know how the scene ended. But the thought of anyone exposing you in any way just infuriated me. I hate to admit it, but I really lost my cool. There were only a few guys that knew we were going to be using the room that night, but when I confronted them, no one was talking," Mike explains on, noticeably rubbing his fist as he recalled the order of events.

"The edited video didn't surface right away and I hoped that it had all just passed. I would always watch your segments on the National Network, and eventually, I convinced myself that you were better off without me in your life. We were actually right where Alec Parker wanted us—apart," he says regretfully then continues.

"Really Sunnie. I still don't know how he did it, who he paid, but we were set–up that night we, uh, picnicked."

"Mike, I have no doubt that Alec used it to keep us apart. I believe you," I say sincerely. My gut, my lips, and my hair are my favorite features; this time, my gut is the chosen one!

"I anticipated this conversation so many times, always hoping that at some point I would at least get to explain my side. I just thought that it would be a harder sell to convince you," Mike says.

"Nope. I believe that true colors will always shine through," I say without any reservation.

"It's that simple?" Mike asks, hoping that it really will be.

"Believing you is that simple. Convincing the rest of society will be the harder part."

"Makes a rough start for me with your family, huh?" Mike asks sounding concerned.

"You want to meet my family?" I perk up with excitement, realizing that he doesn't even filter what he is saying right now.

"I don't mean to scare you or rush anything. I mean I know that we have been living a great distance apart for a while and that I have no idea how much you've moved on, especially when you thought the worst of me. And now, this—finding out this could change everything. Sunnie, I'm scaring you away, right?"

"No, Mike, you are exciting me. My family knows all about you. I talk to them every week even while I have been away. Anyway, they will support me no matter what, I am their Sunnie-girl!"

"We cannot underestimate the shadow this cloud could cast over us if it gets into the wrong hands, Sunnie. I just want to be realistic," Mike says, still sounding concerned.

"Do you have the video?" I ask.

"That's the problem Sunnie; I am not the only one with access to the video. I am so sorry, Sunnie. You have to believe that I could never have been any part of the making of that video."

"I believe you. It's that simple. Stop apologizing. I believe you. Now show me the video."

"Sunnie, you don't want to see it. I was there; I know what happened, but this editing is flawless. It's dark, but it sounds like you, it looks like you...well at least what I imagine the rest of you looks like," Mike smiles to admit that he's never seen me regardless of what everyone else thinks.

"Show me, Mike. I'm okay. Hey, who knows, I may learn something, I'm not as experienced in that department as the world may think," I say with ease and feel no embarrassment for this in front of this amazing guy.

"Wow. So wait a minute, when Alec told me about all of the nights you have been spending with him, he was exaggerating?"

"You mean me and Mr. A-lec-to-exaggerate-how-much-I've-still-got-it-Parker? You must be kidding; he implied that? Hmmm..," I say smiling and drawing in near Mike's face.

"Oh more than implied. He gave me details. I thought of choking him, but it passed," Mike says smoothly.

"Oh really? Why?" I ask.

"Because it made me realize just how much I cared for you and your reputation. And I felt that I had not protected you from him the way I should have. So that's why I wanted to kill him!" Mike explains.

"I actually meant...why did it pass?" I giggle for not stopping him from explaining how much it had bothered him.

Grabbing me in his arms he answers, "I don't really know, Sunnie. We just seemed bigger. I cannot explain it, and I just knew that things would work out for us. I calmed down and left."

Contemplating how to ask or how to best admit that I knew about the security escort, the higher power conversation, and the near strangling already, I reply with a question: "Mike, can you kiss me?" even surprising myself with the details I leave out. I didn't need to ask twice to get double what I had asked for, and like the comfort that had come to Mike, I also just knew that we would work out. The rest, just details.

"I need your help. You have to stay in town longer. Come with me while I film my next segment in the morning. I will figure out a way to sneak you in. You need to be there for this. It will be my last segment; then I will come back home with you."

"I trust you, Sunnie."

"Hi, I'm Sunnie, and you are watching Sunny Side Up brought to you by Farm Fresh Egg Company, serving all continental states. Now you can enjoy farm fresh egg delivery to your doorstep! No matter where you are watching from this morning, you are never far from the farm!"

"Today, I would like to talk to you about a serious matter—one affecting many people thanks to social media. I am risking doing something quite dramatic today for the sake of benefiting many viewers out there. If you are on any type of social media, you may have already seen messages posted asking you to re-post as an experiment to show their teenager how fast something can travel on the internet. This is true!"

"I apologize for all of the suspense surrounding today's topic, but this is something I need to show you. First I will show you a picture of myself that has been cropped and digitally altered. I remember this day well. I was wearing an adorable yellow strapless sundress, I promise, I had my clothes on. Yes, I was kissing this man with my arms wrapped around him; he's my boyfriend. Someone with some mad photo-editing skills was able to crop this photo to exactly where my skin stopped showing, and my sundress started. When paired with the caption above it about Sunnie Grey being spotted with her cameraman near a topless beach, to make it look as if it was some scandalous photo shoot gone wild. I want to prove a point just how easy this can happen, as well as how easily it can spread virally. I also want to mention that it does not even have to be real or true to spread. We were actually not on a topless beach, but instead escaped for only a few minutes to an outside patio breakroom at the station. This was just an example to prove a point how easy it would be to believe the photo."

Just in case you do have any children watching, I want to warn you that the video I will be showing you will be more graphic than the photo. I believe that in the day we live in you need to hear this." For fear of someone cutting the segment off right away for abandoning and changing the script, I wait until the last second to turn my phone around to the video camera. "This is a scandalous sex video of me. I am only showing this from my personal phone, not the station's media equipment. Parents out there watching this segment, I know this is unimaginable to think of, but it happens every day. Young girls are spotted as 'talent' and asked to come in for a quick photo shoot. A small amount of video footage is sometimes enough, if falling in the wrong hands, to end up edited this way. I know that it is small, but I want to go in to show the point where the editing starts. Here you see me kissing my boyfriend, and next you see a woman of a similar look and build, removing all clothing. Okay, and I will stop right here. My viewers all have an imagination, right?" I smile into the camera giving the audience the credit of handling a mature topic. "Look, you all know how

I love attempting to help people have a sunnier day in simple steps, but sometimes we have to be able to go deeper, into harder topics. We can still use very simple steps for our safety and reputation. These things can happen to anyone, but hopefully, by me sharing this mock-demonstration we have created for you today, I have helped you think about your own simple steps toward internet safety! Please continue to enjoy posting about your sunny days. Thanks for tuning in!"

"Cut. Sunnie, you are...I don't really know what to say," Robert delivers, shaking his head.

"It's okay; you let me finish," I say with a smile, and move toward the back of the room to find Mike.

"Sunnie's got a boyfriend...wha-wha!" Gregory starts with the chanting as I pass him. Though he missed the point completely, he sure breaks the tension.

"What did you think?" I say while throwing my arms around Mike.

"I think...that you will never stop surprising me. You always find another angle to view every situation, don't you, Sun?"

"There always is another angle; maybe I just point it out," I say with a quick kiss.

"True, my girlfriend," Mike laughs hugging me.

"Oh, did you like that boyfriend stuff?" I giggle.

"Don't read your messages now, every guy in America will be complaining to hear that Sunnie has a boyfriend!" Mike teases.

"Oh, funny."

"No joke, there is someone coming in that will definitely be complaining. Turn around because here comes your friend."

Mike respectfully addresses Alec when he approaches, "I'm sorry, Mr. Parker. I know you asked me not to be in the building just yesterday. I will go now. I just came by the station to say goodbye."

"It's okay. Sunnie, your boyfriend, can stay," Alec pauses before speaking again then heading out of the room. "Sunnie, I need to speak with you in private."

Feeling calm and light to have this chapter in my life closing, I am so grateful to have learned so

much. I just want to go home to my family. I kiss
Mike goodbye promising to wrap things up here
and get home soon. I could tell that he was hesitant
for me to meet with Alec alone, but it was
necessary.

All I hope to accomplish in Alec's office is an amicable resignation, with little drama in my professional record. I could pick up on my old position at the rehab center that I had before I ever landed the segment on the show. I am a different Sunnie than the sunny girl I was before I was chosen for the "Sunny Side Up" Segment. I think back to all of the faces of the people I helped there. Those recovering from hip replacements that loved having this hip girl with a smile always trying to provide encouragement and make their day better.

Who says you can't go home? So I had a taste of making people's days with a bigger audience, then even a broader viewer base with the National segment, but I can go back home and concentrate on making people's recoveries smoother, and brighter! First I must resign from this position of making people's days brighter on the air, before they blow out my light, and fire me!

Maybe I should have rehearsed this before just bursting in his office already speaking, "First Alec; I want to say that I never meant to disrespect you or anyone at either station by hi-jacking today's segment with an unapproved one. I saw a big problem for me with that video possibly being in the wrong hands, and I was not just acting selfishly, I care about the station's credibility and reputation as well. And yes, I even care about the ratings. I felt that I needed to protect myself, and now I will resign and let the next, and likely more trainable, IT girl take over managing the ratings," I say sadly, but knowing that it is the right thing to do.

"Oh no, you don't, Sunnie. You don't just get to say what you want and then leave. If I taught you only one thing in all of this time, please let it be that you understand consequences to every action. Even the slightest changes have affected ratings in the past. Tell me that you understand at least this much?"

"I do, I am sorry," Despite feeling grateful to this man who has taught me so much, when factoring in all of the other lessons that he has taught me from his actions, I cannot just forgive and forget again, enabling him to treat me inappropriately behind closed doors.

"Sunnie, I accept your apology on behalf of the station, but you are going to listen to what I have to say. You were young, you were completely inexperienced in this business, and quite frankly we took a risk on you. You have shown little regard to what we think of you or how we have tried to curve you into the IT girl that we wanted you to be. Do you know how many millions of young women would do anything to have your job, Sunnie? The internet has allowed anyone to become a star, but only long enough for someone to get a taste for it, a high that doesn't last but leaves the person desperate for that next approval. The typical fifteen minutes of fame has been reduced to five minutes if that! But Sunnie you take it all for granted. You worry so little about staying but yet, like the sun, just keep coming up again. I've never seen this." "You changed the way we all see this business. You are not leaving us, Sunnie. We will not accept your resignation. In fact, we are the putty in your hands, mold us into what you want from the station. Keep us brighter Sunnie, would you? Make us the tool to make America brighter, even when we face difficult times in our country's history. I don't know what, Sunnie. Maybe homelessness & poverty, natural disasters, wounded warriors & veterans, terrorist threats, heroin addiction, obesity, soaring divorce rates, depression, anything Sunnie. Use the sunny way, your "Sunnie-way", to make the slightest difference to our viewers all across the country," Alec says, sounding like he actually wants to believe in all of this, not just about the ratings, but the segments actually brightening someone's life. Could this be?

Alec continues, "Already Sunnie, it's the most hits on our network in history. You have built that viewer base, you have been their sunny girl. You are not only America's sweetheart...you are brightening America. Now you have taken it to the next level. By you taking it a step deeper, you have just given real, sincere hope and advice to viewers."

With barely a pause, Alec begins again. "Certainly not a topic that any of us in the business would have advised you to take on, especially not in the first time going deep with your viewers. Maybe it's your higher power thing that you and your little boyfriend keep talking of. I don't know, Sunnie, where that light comes from, but America sees it," Alec says, shaking his head.

"And by the way, if that cocky man of yours should not take his position as your boyfriend seriously, you let me know, and I will fire him in that department and from the camera crew."

"Wait, Mike still has a job back at home at the station?" I ask with surprise.

"Yes, along with a few other things that he will enjoy. You two have already been requested to film a half hour segment on the national network on internet safety for teens," Alec continues.

"Oh, Alec!" Without even thinking through our history, I jump in his arms, making two initial observations. One, he smells as nice as ever and two, his hug is appropriate. The second one I just have to comment on, commenting on the first one, I know would be a bad idea. "Alec, you give an amazing, appropriate hug! Who knew?" I joke.

"Don't stay in my arms too long sweet, naive girl, I mean I am Mr. A-lec-to-grab-a-feel-Parker, right Sunnie? Is that similar to the names you like to make up in the break room?" he teases.

"Oh, you know about those kind of names. I'm sorry," I say, a bit embarrassed. "Since you brought that up, Alec, I would actually like to call you Mr. Parker when I address you in all situations, public and behind the scenes.

"So Sunnie, what do you say? What can we do to keep you on our team?" Alec pleas.

"Okay, we all know that I am better on the spot, so here goes. I believe the segment can be filmed anywhere and then broadcast nationally. I want to go back with you to my home set. I want to be with the old crew, including Mike. I want to sit in Sam's hair and make-up chair every day. I want to work with Jazzy and the wardrobe team and have more of a say in my clothing selections ahead of time. I want a smoothie machine in the break room. And no matter what, good or bad segments, I will have you respect me, which means no touchy, feely stuff on the side. You do realize that with your leadership and zero tolerance, there would be a lot less of that type of behavior among the crew as well. And Alec, I mean Mr. Parker, not even for a special segment will anyone make me announce fake eggs; THAT would truly make me crack!"

I continue, aware that I am babbling in all of my excitement, "This may seem petty, and we can talk more about this later, but there is a segment that I wrote about 'Helpies', which are basically Selfies, only with two people instead of just oneself. To me, it only makes sense to have both people engaged in the moment and the work of collecting the perfect photo, you know, heads up and focused, with both people looking in the right direction. I have no idea why this segment didn't get approved in the first place? I really think the term 'Helpie' can take off and even help other people with this new concept, you know? Oh, never mind, it sounds crazy when I explain it here."

Done thinking, but unfortunately not done talking, after a breath I continue rambling on with the same momentum. "There may be some other items that I am not thinking of at the moment, but I think that will do for now!" I smile at his amused face while shaking Alec's hand. "Complete relocation fees and airfare, just an understood, right?"

"Of course, Sunnie. We have to keep you happy to keep America happy!" Alec laughs.

"Wait, that makes it sound like I am just some spoiled diva demanding everything she wants on the set, right?" I question.

"Certainly not, I didn't mean it that way. You demand the kind of things that no one else ever thought to, you are a one-of-a-kind-talent!"

"Wait, Alec, uh, I mean Mr. Parker, I despise being called talent...it seems so replaceable. I should have said that after the first segment," I remember hearing that in my first several after-segment-critiques with his hand on my ass!

"Note taken, Sunnie! It is just lingo of the business, but you are not so easily replaceable!"

"Actually, Mr. Parker, anyone could probably do my job, the difference is just that I know I can." Stepping out the door and into the hallway ready to scream with excitement, I hear Alec call for me again. I pop my head back in to hear the nicest words yet.

"Sunnie, I happen to know that Mike's plane doesn't leave for another couple of hours. He rode the group shuttle to the airport, so if you go now by car, you could probably catch him. Maybe have a picnic with him before he goes. I hear that's what you kids love to do together." Funny that Alec sounds like he truly wants the best for me, almost fatherly even.

"Mike, Mike," I call out as soon as I spot him, thanking God that I found him without a cell phone! My clean car never traveled so fast on the freeway before today.

"Good thing you found me, I was just about to go through the gates and get something to eat on the other side," Mike says sounding relieved and picking me up from the ground.

"Well, you are in luck! You get me and some food," I say. "It's not fancy, just some sandwiches that I snagged from a tray, brought in for someone's meeting at the station today. It will make for a nice picnic."

"You have the best ideas, I still remember from your picnicking segment months ago," Mike laughs.

"Actually, it was Alec's idea," I say which halts his laughter.

"No kidding. Are you sure mine is not poisoned?" Mike asks teasing.

"Oh no, no worries, I have all kinds of news in that department, but first, let's get all set up here. I'm so happy to be on a date with you, out in public!"

"A quick airport date in three simple steps!" Mike laughs and tickles me.

"Stop playing and eat. Let's make the most of our time!" I warn him, but I am really not upset at all. I am fine doing anything with this man.

So I want to know...the other night, before the day I came to your set, you mentioned that you had finally called me? What did you call me for anyway?" Mike asked.

"Well I wasn't calling you for video work, that's for sure," I laugh, though it's not entirely funny.

"Seriously, why did you call? And after all that time?" Mike asks.

"Well I never finished telling you about my name," I say, feeling a little silly. I would feel even sillier if I had to admit that I was using that name thing as a reason to call.

"About your name?" Mike asks.

"You know, a long time ago you had asked me about my name," I reply.

"Oh yeah, Sunnie Grey, your stage name," Mike teases.

"My real name, thank you! Now you are going to have to worry about starting off bad with my family if they hear you say that!" I giggle.

"So tell me, Miss Grey? How did you get your sunny little first name? Was it sunny outside when you were born?"

"No, it was nighttime," I answer.

"It was sunny out when you were conceived?" Mike asks.

"Oh my! No, it was probably nighttime then too," I add.

"Oh, you had the kind of parents who only have sex at night?"

"No, I mean I don't know. Who knows when their parents have sex? Really Mike? You are getting me way off topic!" I say while playfully hitting him.

"Let me guess; they didn't have a name, and the local weatherman stepped in to help?" Mike laughs harder.

"Can you be serious? If you just stop guessing, I will tell you," I say.

"Okay, okay. Please tell me, Miss Grey."

"My parents were on a camping trip when I came into the world. They were out in the middle of nowhere, and the only thing near was an Indian Reservation. The Indian that helped my Mother with the delivery of me was given the right to name me."

"Sunnie, that is so crazy. Where was your father?" Mike looks shocked.

"Oh he was right there, but he was busy learning a rain dance. Ironic, huh?" I smile.

"How 'bout it?" Mike comments, clearly not knowing what to say.

"Well now you know," I say, grinning hugely while he has a chance to think through it.

"Sunnie, are you messing with me?" Mike asks.

"It was my turn!" I laugh.

"Now how will I know if I can trust you?" Mike asks with his arms wrapped around me again.

"I guess you will just have to believe in me, nothing you haven't put me through!" I tease.

"Well just to be sure I can, I am going to have to change your name," Mike adds.

"Change my name? You can't just change my name," I say, confused with his crazy ideas.

"Yes, I will. And I may not take no for an answer," Mike announces with certainty.

"Miss Sunnie Grey, would you please agree to change your name to Mrs. Sunnie Wright, therefore making me the happiest man alive?" Mike says with the nicest, most sincere smile I have ever seen on anyone. I say nothing and stare back at him. "Okay, I see this is going to be harder than I thought IF I agree to get down on one knee, will you please agree to change your name?"

"Yes. I will change my name! I will change my name to yours. I will join you, and all that comes with it!"

"So you will marry me, My Sunnie?" Mike says, apparently just wanting to hear it all again.

"Well, now you are pushing it! I only agreed to change my name. You don't even think that you have a job, do you?" I smile, waiting for him to respond to that, but instead he drops to one knee, lifting my hand to his lips. "Of course, you crazy man, I will marry you," I announce.

"I knew after the first two minutes with you that this was eventually going to happen. For you, Sunnie...I am and will always be...Mr. RIGHT!"

Mike says cockily, pulling me down to sit on his outstretched knee.

"Really, and how did you know?" I can't help but giggle, knowing this is right and that he is Mr. Right. I am going to be Mrs. Wright!

"I just did, Sunnie. You felt it too." Mike kisses my forehead, lifts us both back up and picks up his bags to go. Neither of us gives much attention to the crowd drawing around to witness an airport proposal. Who cares if they are gawking, or even have their cell phones in hand capturing it all!

"You're Sunnie, right?" someone calls out with excitement, recognizing me from the show.

"Yes, I am," I answer, amused that she was onto more than she even knew with her question. I cannot wait to be able to answer that same question with: "Yes, I am Sunnie Wright!"

"We love you! We watch you all the time!" she and her friend call over to me. "Sunnie can we have you sign something for us?"

I notice others perk up as well and figure out quickly that if I say, "yes" that I am going to be here awhile. I turn to look at Mike and then back to the crowd. Nothing in Mike's look gave me a clue at all of what to do. He is my Mr. Right, allowing me to choose how to navigate through this public life that I am living all in attempts to brighten people's days.

"Yes, of course, I will," I say in the direction of the crowd, "but first I need a private moment for a quick farewell conversation. What can I say...I seem to be on a real 'yes' roll lately?" I turn my attention back to Mike, and with a much quieter voice, I tell him goodbye.

"I have some more Yes's for you, Mike, and then I know you have to go," I say.

"More yes's?" Mike asks.

"As I said...I am on a roll. Yes, I will be on a plane later this week. Yes, it will be permanent and not just a visit. Yes, I will be working at the station doing what I love, and yes, I will be doing it in front of my favorite cameraman! We will both be working for Mr. Parker in the same town," I say as I throw my arms around him. "Hearing me address the boss as Mr. Parker, I know that must sound strange! I have so much more to tell you, but anyway he will make everything happen for me to film nationally from our home station, and yes it is true, with you in your favorite position on the crew."

"Sunnie, before I take off you should know... I'm...I'm falling more in love with you."

"Wow, I will have to give yes's more often!"

"I am serious. You are my Sun. I have no idea where you were before you brightened up everything in my world, but I never want to live in a place without your rays."

"Well, we'll talk about all of that 'before stuff' at a later time, I am the one who is lucky to have ended up in your world somehow. I'm in love with you too, Mike. Goodbye for now in three easy steps," I say with a kiss between each step and of course ending with my signature wink—this wink just for him. "Kiss, wave, and get home safely!" Though we are not on-air, I think it is the best segment I have ever written!

"Hi, I'm Sunnie, and you are watching Sunny Side Up brought to you by Farm Fresh Egg Company, serving all continental states. Now you can enjoy farm fresh egg delivery to your doorstep! Even if you are watching from the airport this afternoon, you are never far from the farm! Just kidding. I just thought that if you have taken the time to wait, then you should get some of what you love me for!" I deliver to a crowd of amused smiles, before reaching out my hand to grab items to sign. Several papers, notebooks, journal books, t-shirts, a keychain, and a yellow sunshine luggage tag later, I head out of the airport feeling a mix of excitement and exhaustion. But with no surprise to me when I glide through the last door, I am greeted by a very sunny day. Thanks for tuning in Mr. Sun. Everyone else is squinting from his brightness, but I wink at him before putting on my shades.

About the Author

Award-winning fiction author, SC Russell, was born in New York and raised in Ohio. SC currently resides in Cincinnati with her husband and two children with the perk of many grandparents nearby to spoil, enjoy, and build into them!

SC has a passion for writing adult contemporary fiction and children's books as a second career.

She studied in a Psychology Program at Bowling Green State University, and then in a Graduate Program at Xavier University, followed by numerous years of experience in counseling. SC has always concerned herself with how people feel about themselves and their surroundings.

With the desire to be a positive influence to others in person, as well as through her writing, SC will continue to spread an optimistic attitude throughout her message.

SC loves to travel and is most often a destination writer—known for always completing the last writing of each book at an inspirational and peaceful location. SC has an enthusiastic desire to visit and appreciate all National Parks in the USA. She also enjoys: spending time with friends & family, reading as many books as possible, biking tandem with hubby, kayaking on the Great Lakes, swimming in an endless pool while watching the sunrise, and cooking healthy, exciting internationally-themed-meals to ensure that the memories of all the countries visited as a family remains alive in her children forever!